ALSO BY T.M. BASHFORD

The Tide Series

The Forbidden Tide (Book 2)

The Chilling Tide (Book 3)

Novella

Becoming Sienna

I0626045

PRAISE FOR THE TIDE SERIES

"It's been a long while since I was up all hours of the night with my nose stuck in a book, unable to put it down . . . very visual and colourful . . . with a magnetic twist." *Sandra Severgnini, Author & Illustrator*

"Mesmerising. T.M. Bashford is my new favorite author." *Amazon Reviewer.*

"It's so refreshing to read about a strong, yet realistic and complex female character." *Goodreads Reviewer.*

"There were moments my heart rate spiked up to 100 bpm (per my fitbit) . . . so many spots kept me turning the pages into the wee hours of the morning." *Avid Romance Reader, Amber Truelson*

THE
HEARTLESS
TIDE

T. M. BASHFORD

THE HEARTLESS TIDE

This book is a work of fiction. Names, places, characters, and incidents are the product of the author's imagination or are used fictitiously.

Print: ISBN-13: 978-0-6486780-1-4

Digital ISBN-13: 978-0-6486780-0-7

Cover Design: Blue Water Books

Editor: Silvia Curry

Library of Congress Control Number: 2020900117

A catalogue record for this work is available from the National Library of Australia

For women everywhere who fall for the wrong guy . . .
before finding the right one.

CHAPTER 1

I wake to the sound of the rigging flick-flacking in the bony pre-dawn light. My neck is cricked from falling asleep in the cockpit. The boat lolls gently in the ocean, and the limp sails hang like a blouse, half-fallen from a coat hanger. In the distance, the island of Western Samoa is a dark, squiggly line on the horizon.

I've made it all the way from California.

Two months alone at sea.

A blond sun creeps higher into the sky and bathes all thirty-four feet of *Sassy Jam* in pale yellow light. When the wind changes, I tack closer to the island. My long hair streaks behind me, a scarf the shade of wet tea leaves.

Samoa is the color of holidays. White-washed villa walls and tan beaches form the backdrop to the swaying jade of the palms and a rainbow of blues. The view surprises my eyes after being at sea for so long—like a blind person all at once gaining their sight. I almost forget my fear of being forced ashore.

But I have no choice. I must take the risk.

I inflate the dinghy, then reach for my hoodie to disguise

myself. The zipped pocket bulges with the wad of cash to pay for boat repairs. *The last person to touch that money is dead.*

Small boulders pepper the shoreline. I navigate the dinghy around them, paddling with two locker doors I'd detached from the boat. I lost the oars at sea. In the shallows, I pull the dinghy onto the sand, then tie it to a palm tree. I doubt myself for what I'm about to do. But without the windvane, I'll have to steer manually for the final few weeks to Australia and that could be hazardous—I wouldn't be able to do repairs, cook, pee, or rest. It would slow me down too, making it easier for them to catch up with me.

I've anchored far from the main harbor, unwilling to risk an encounter with customs, and now I have a long walk ahead of me. The edges of the tarmac bleed into ginger dust, and a hand-painted sign confirms I'm in Valusu Bay. To reach the street, I hop from one rounded boulder to another, flip-flops in hand so that my bare feet can nuzzle the warm rocks, but it's impossible not to sway after being at sea for two months.

My hoodie hides my face and hair but sweat slicks my skin. I ponder the deserted road. A ripple of nerves makes me hesitate, but then I shrug off the hoodie and tie it around my waist.

As the sun rises in the sky, and I get closer to Apia, the volume of people and vehicle traffic builds. Staccato blasts of noise clang and hurt my ears—I've grown used to the soft sounds of the ocean.

A gong sounds from a local hotel and a cluster of stray dogs bark and scatter. My stomach prickles with nerves. The gong appears to be a lunch bell, but it's a reminder I should be watching for police and searching for someone to fix *Sassy's* windvane. Except, I don't know who to trust. A boat builder might want my non-existent customs papers and passport.

Maybe I should return to *Sassy Jam.*

The aroma of freshly cooked pork on spits at the entrance to a fish market makes my mouth water. Stalling, I resolve to eat a proper meal before deciding on anything.

After ordering, I throw my flip-flops on the dirt floor under a table in the corner and attempt to be invisible while I watch the busy market from behind the safety of my hair which falls forward like a curtain.

The pork arrives in a bowl, drowning in spicy-smelling coconut milk. After the bland tins of fish and freeze-dried foods on *Sassy*, the flavors are intense bursts of tanginess on my tongue and I don't eat in a lady-like fashion. Like a starving person, I eat with my fingers—using a knife and fork is too finicky and would take too long. I inhale the meat, savoring the flavors. Streaky spinach drips coconut milk down my chin, so when I wipe my chin with my wrist, I spread the mess farther.

"Not eaten for a month?"

My gaze cuts across the café tables and lands on a couple of Western guys who must've just sat down. They stare at me with laughing eyes. I fight the impulse to spin away. Men always make me feel as if I'm the gazelle and they're the lion. But today, the hunted feeling quickly dwindles. The guy with light-brown hair intrigues me because of his feet—his long legs stretch out under his table, crossed at the ankles, and he's barefoot, his soles blackened. I glance down at my own feet. My boyfriend, Connor, used to rebuke me for never wearing shoes, calling me his 'brown-soled girl' rather than his 'brown-eyed girl' from the song.

Used to rebuke me.

Intrigued, I examine this man's face. His amused eyes are an unusual ultramarine blue. His smile widens, and it's like opening a porthole on a breathtaking view. I put down the bowl, desperate for some sort of napkin. I should use my hoodie.

"You need one of these." The second, dark-haired guy

saunters toward me, waving a paper napkin that will be as much use as a chocolate hairdryer at this point.

I spring to my feet. He's one of those male strutters you see at the gym, overly proud of his height and muscles. He has olive-colored skin and dark, almost black eyes, like mine. His eyebrows are bushy and his mouth is twisted into an undying smirk.

When I don't take the napkin, he puts it on the table. I pause, clear my throat, and snatch it up to wipe my chin. It's instantly soggy. My cheeks heat to lollipop red when I peel it away.

"Might need about a hundred of them," I mumble.

"Happy to oblige." He performs a theatrical half-bow.

I cringe, recognizing his overbearing helpfulness from some of the men I've come across at sailing meets or when teaching guys to sail—flirts on the lookout for sex, not friendship. He strides to the counter with its peeling Formica top and dimpled metal panels while I stay trapped in the spotlight of Blue Eyes' gaze.

The sultry sun squats on my neck. I try not to fidget and stare at my dirty feet. "Have I turned red yet?" I murmur, more to myself.

"You've got a pretty dark tan there, which is doing a good job of hiding it. Well, *most* of it." Humor gathers in his eyes like bright sunshine bursting into a room. I recognize his accent—Australian.

Usually, I'd let my hair fall across my face, but now everything is sticky—mouth, chin, cheeks, fingers, wrists. I wish there was a way to speed up time, or swallow it, or pour it away.

"Not sure I've seen your style of eating before. Very . . . becoming," he teases.

I try for a sharp retort, but there's only the awkwardness of silence. I've never been much of a talker, and I've always been a loner, preferring boats to people. Everyone thinks it's because I'm shy. I'm not. It's just easier to keep family secrets that way. Besides, men are circling sharks. They might laugh and joke on the outside—as my father had, as Connor had—but behind that is a whole secret men's world I'll never trust again.

Under the heat of Blue Eyes' contemplation, I watch my toes curl into the dirt, hoping he's not trying to remember where he's seen me before. After another awkward few seconds, I scan the market next to the café. The tourists are obvious in their shorts and T-shirts, yet they mingle with Polynesian girls in floaty dresses who flit down narrow streets, resembling colorful butterflies. My usual denim shorts and tank top put me in the invisible tourist camp.

The dark-haired guy chats at the counter as if he has all the time in the world. A hot breeze lifts the plastic table-cloths, each with a rock the size of my fist in its center to hold the checked cloth down. The metallic stench of the fish market thrusts up my nose. I push down on the fluster inside. Except, I can't bear waiting another moment and grab my hoodie, using it to clean myself up.

"Here you go, gorgeous." The dark-haired guy hands over a bundle of paper napkins.

I take them, wishing I could turn myself into a table. "Thanks."

"Perhaps we can join you and show you how to eat that pork . . . it's tricky." He's standing too close. "We prefer to use things called a knife and fork." He lays a knife in front of me, followed by a fork.

I let my hair fall over my face, place the napkins on my bowl, and tie the hoodie around my waist.

"Leave her alone, Brett." Blue Eyes rests both arms on the table and spins the lid from his water bottle. "Sorry," he adds, "Brett thinks he's being charming. And he can never resist a pretty face." His voice is playful, matching the gaze he's locked me in. His eyes are more of a steel blue now, made extra intense by his tanned skin and aqua T-shirt which stretches across wide shoulders. I pray for something clever —actually anything—to say, but after weeks alone, my tongue can't keep up with the thoughts that jig in my head. Then again, I've never been able to talk to men.

Instinct tells me to get going in case they recognize me from a news story.

"I gotta go." I bend to pick up the flip-flops at the same time Brett stoops to retrieve them. When he pauses and stares at my tattoo—a delicate gray, white, and taupe sea eagle that soars above my ankle bone—I panic that it's an identifying feature and might have been on the news stories. I jerk to conceal it and we knock heads. Brett falls back onto his butt, dramatically rubbing his temple.

"I'm sorry," I say, clipped. He takes my offered hand and huffs into a chair, head bent low between his forearms. "Did it hurt that much? You must have a skull made of mango." Finally, some words trip off my tongue.

Blue Eyes laughs, balancing on the back legs of his chair. "She's got you there, mate." His Aussie accent is faintly posh.

"Busted," Brett says. He sits upright and regards me through a dark, floppy fringe. "So, what's an American fashion model like you doing all the way out here?"

My tongue baffles around inside my mouth. I blink at his friend. Our eyes collide. *Whoa!* Something in my chest flutters, a tell-tale ribbon.

"I'm just seeing a bit of the world," I reply.

"Drew and I have traveled all over America." He flicks his chin toward Blue Eyes—Drew—and back again. "Where do you call home?"

I recall how, after the death of my boyfriend's parents last year, Connor and I had moved into Stratton Hall in a very exclusive part of Malibu, and how at the age of twenty-two, I'd finally felt grown up. *I got that completely wrong.* Now, I suppress an image of the iron entrance gates of Stratton Hall

6

on that final day—how they'd reeled ajar and clanged shut in the wind. I should've known Connor had snuck home early to check up on me.

"California," I say. "Are you Australian?" I direct my question at Drew. I guess he's a similar age to me.

Time hangs. As if I asked him for his phone number.

"Yup. From Sydney," he says.

The sun has given his hair highlights and it spikes up around the front. *Holy hair! He's not some piece of art in a museum.* I didn't know I could be so . . . *Emily-like.* Emily, my roommate in college, had been boy-crazy.

I put my reaction to this man down to being alone at sea for so long.

"How long you been traveling?" Drew asks, still fiddling with the bottle top.

"Couple of months."

"On your own?" Brett drinks me in like he wants to guzzle me up.

I take a small backward step. *They're asking too many questions.* "Anyhow. Nice meeting you both, but I gotta go."

"Sure Vega and I can't interest you in something more deluxe than a bottle of water?" Brett presses.

"Vega? I thought it was Drew?" I frown at Drew.

"Drew Vega," Brett cuts in.

"Like the brightest star in the northern constellation of—" I pause. *Now there's an apt name.*

Drew cocks his head. "How'd you know that? Most people make jokes about ninjas in that Street Fighter game, but I'm sadly lacking the claw, mask, snake tattoo, and ponytail, so that joke kinda falls flat."

"Or the *Pulp Fiction* movie reference," interrupts Brett, but he's receded into the background—even the volume of his voice appears dimmer.

"Vega. Part of the Lyra constellation and the Summer Triangle," I finish.

"Are you into astronomy or, don't tell me, astrology?" Drew asks.

No, I'm a fugitive who uses the stars to navigate. Suddenly shy and wishing I'd kept my mouth shut, I repeat, "I gotta go."

Brett steps forward, blocking Drew. "What's with the hoodie, Gotta Go Girl? It's insanely hot today." A muscle in his jaw twitches. Connor's jaw would twitch when he got frustrated and was about to get angry. Same with my dad—it all of a sudden seems like a silent warning.

I push the chair under the table. "Always be prepared."

Drew gives me a casual wave. "You didn't tell us your name."

My brain cringes. What if I'm headlining on every news website? Shae Love is an easy name to remember. "Emily." The name of my old college roommate blurts into the space between us. "I gotta go. I need to find a boatyard."

"I'm sure we could help you find one," Brett jumps in.

No. I crouch to fetch my flip-flops. "It's okay. I'll find one."

"Are you buying a boat?"

"Maybe."

"Let her go, Brett," Drew says. "Although, if you don't have any luck, Emily, I know this guy. He's from England. There's nothing he doesn't know about boats. He sails them, builds them, fixes them. He can spot a dud from a hundred feet." Drew's open smile makes me want to trust him.

I pause. They're just being helpful. Friendly. But I hate owing favors because what will they want in return? I head to the counter to pay, ignoring Brett's begging.

After spending two months alone at sea, I've had ample time to think about my life choices, and one of them is that all men are off-limits. I plan to stick to boats. I often replayed a conversation I had with Emily after being ribbed for not having a boyfriend in college—before I met Connor Stratton.

"One day you'll understand what you're missing," my friend had said. "It's as if I'm only a whole person when I'm with Rick, and I'm happy just being with him—even watching football."

"You're only half a person without him?" I replied.

"Possibly. Maybe that's what love is—finding your other half."

I had doubted Emily. If you needed a guy to make you feel whole, then you relied on them too much and when they started beating up on you, you couldn't leave. My mother had needed my father so much that she took everything he handed out with his fists. But I hadn't told a soul about that family secret—wife-beating didn't happen in stockbroker families who sent their children to private school, were members of an exclusive yacht club, and were part of the Malibu glitterati. I had simply told Emily that I'd rather have a boat than a boyfriend.

"But you can't cuddle a boat," Emily replied.

"I wouldn't say that. My boats and I are very close."

Back then, I had been so sure. So strong. If only I'd stuck to that philosophy. Then everything with Connor would never have happened.

In the moment I crossed the equator with *Sassy Jam,* I had emptied a tin of tuna into the sea as a sacrifice and tribute to Neptune, something my father had once told me about. Then I anointed myself by pouring a bucket of Southern Hemisphere ocean water over myself as a sort of ritual to mark the fact that I'd joined the rank of shellbacks with so many other sailors. And then I vowed to never fall in love again.

CHAPTER 2

A woman in the nearby food market screams as I exit the café. My heart bounces in my ribcage. I get set to run. But the woman isn't looking at me. She's gaping at a caramel-colored dog, its jaw attached to her ankle. A low growl slips between its bared teeth.

Drew jumps the stumpy wooden fence that separates the café from the street. He's holding a bowl and tips it at the dog's feet. The mutt releases his hold and gobbles up the morsel while the woman, who looks like a tourist, stumbles backward, whimpering and tripping. I straddle the fence, intending to help her, but the woman panics and yanks me down next to her. The dog jerks and bares its teeth at us. It has a bloodied gash across the top of its head and comes closer to sniff my sauce-covered hoodie. I throw the hoodie aside to distract it.

Drew steps between the dog and me, bends to grab something from the ground, and goes to fling it at the dog. The stray stiffens, whips round, and scampers away, tail between its legs.

I clamber to my feet. "What did you throw at it?"

"Nothing. I pretended to throw a rock. That makes them take off." Drew turns to the shaking tourist, her teased blond hair-do now lopsided.

"My ankle. I can't put weight . . ." Her accent suggests she's from America.

"Let me take a look, okay?" Drew says. He glances at the retreating dog, then squats beside her.

"Thank you. I thought he was going to bite my foot off. Vicious brute."

"He was hungry and must've gotten spooked," Drew mumbles. 'What's your name?'

"Sigourney." The woman rests a heavy hand on Drew's stooped back.

I retrieve my hoodie and hover, as futile as a one-knot wind at sea, while Drew inspects Sigourney's ankle. I stand to the side of them in case the woman recognizes me from a US news broadcast.

Drew adds, "You should go to a hospital. Get this cleaned up and have some shots."

"I can clean myself up." She lifts her foot and winces. "Who does the mutt belong to?"

Drew ignores the question. "If the dog is rabid, you will need a tetanus shot, or you could end up seriously ill, dead even. Are you here with anyone?"

The woman's mouth pinches. "My husband's playing golf. I can't reach him for hours."

Drew studies Brett, who's watching from the café. "Can you make a trip to the hospital with Sigourney, Brett?"

Brett glugs the last of his water. Smirking, he rummages in his pocket then jangles a bunch of keys which he points at the offending stray dog. "Don't tell me, another dog to save?"

When Brett drives away with his passenger, Drew's gaze cuts to me "You okay?"

His voice is soft, private. I can't remember the last time, if ever, I was spoken to so tenderly. A lightbulb switches on inside my chest.

"You owe me a drink, though," he adds. "You were nearly dog food." He's holding in a smile when he glances up the road. The stray's almost out of sight. "Did you see the dog's head? Someone's put an elastic band around it as a make-shift muzzle. But the band's cutting into her flesh. I might need your help. Before she gets herself into more trouble. Just a few minutes. Poor thing can't be expected to be in a good mood, can she?" Drew's already turning to leave before he finishes the question, as if he's not expecting me to refuse.

I open my mouth to object but know I can't walk away as if I don't care about the dog—as if he hasn't asked for my help. And if I go with him, I might figure out if he's trust-worthy and if this English boat expert is for real. How bad can a guy who helps a stranger be? And it'd be an exchange of favors—Drew's help in exchange for my help with the dog. Then I don't owe him anything.

Drew's pace picks up into a trot. I scramble after him, but he stops so abruptly I run into the back of him, biting the inside of my mouth.

"Jeez, sorry. Didn't realize you were there." He grabs my upper arms to steady me. His lips twitch with humor, but his expression shows concern.

"My fault." I keep my focus on the dog, pretending the collision never happened.

The stray mopes past various stalls, sniffing at bins before it pees in a bush. Drew enters the kiosk next to us to buy a bag of chips. He crinkles the bag noisily, eyeing the dog who stares intently at the chip bag. Drew tilts his head to beckon me but pops into another stall, pushing through a doorway framed by multi-colored dresses. I wait outside, feeling like a spare part.

When he comes out, he passes me a leather belt. "Can you hold this?"

I'm so grateful to be useful my face busts into a ridiculous grin. "Shopping? At a time like this?" I'm shocked by my teasing tone.

"It's an addiction," he jokes, "I'm getting help for it."

We engage in another brief staring competition. I scold myself for being an Emily.

"Stay back for now, okay?" Drew takes off his T-shirt, revealing a broad tanned back that narrows into a slim waist. He tucks the shirt into the side of his khaki shorts and his six-pack flexes. *Can this situation get any more awkward?* I tie my hoodie around my middle.

Drew sidles closer to the dog. Scrunching the chip bag, he opens it, eats a couple, and purposely drops some on the floor. The mutt stops in her tracks and stares from Drew to the fallen chips and back again. Drew munches on more chips, spilling a few more and stepping a few paces away before repeating his actions. The dog takes a wary step forward.

Slowly reaching for his T-shirt, Drew winds it around his left hand. He breathes in deeply a couple of times, and I can't help but stare at his naked torso, at the light smattering of blond hair covering his pecs. The dog gobbles the chips until she's eating at Drew's feet. With the wrapped hand, Drew rubs the dog's back, inches above her tail. The contact makes the dog flinch. Her tail sinks between her back legs, which slacken. She growls.

"Ah, ah," Drew says sharply, showing the mutt who's boss. The dog stops grumbling, and Drew moves his left hand near her nose. She sniffs the T-shirt, growling. "Ah, ah." He pets the stray's back more forcefully, moves up until he's rubbing her neck. "Good girl." Drew's voice is calm and soft now, rewarding the dog. Her tail lifts as she gives a small wag. "You're okay. I'm not going to hurt you." Drew beckons me, points at the belt. I match his quiet manner and edge closer.

"Can you loop it so I can use it as a leash?" His speech is

hushed, hypnotic. I do as he asks, and he slips the belt around the dog's neck.

"Are you some sort of dog whisperer?" I ask.

Or a real-life Captain America.

Drew laughs, feeding the stray more chips. "I work at the animal shelter. There are more stray dogs in Samoa than there are tourists." He stoops to stroke the dog, adding, "Can you see the elastic band?"

I inspect the dog. Something is cutting into the flesh across the top of her head.

"It's so tight I can't get rid of it." Drew rubs an eyebrow with his knuckle. "It's a cruel muzzle. But thanks for your help."

"I didn't do much." I will myself to focus on his face rather than his bare chest and abs. As Drew holds my gaze, it's as if my heart is being wrestled to the ground and pinned there.

Pulsing.

I'd crewed on boats at the yacht club with shirtless men before, but they'd never made me react like this.

"Most girls would've found an excuse about a hair appointment or something," he says before he throws down more chips. "I'm going to walk her to the shelter. I can't take the band off myself, and I doubt this dog's into taxi rides." He flashes a crooked grin. "It's fifteen minutes away. You can come if you want . . ."

My insides curl.

But would he be asking me to tag along if he knew what I'd done to Connor? The image of Connor's body slumped outside the kitchen, his bloody handprints marking the door, slams into my head.

I look back toward the harbor.

Drew adds, "I forgot . . . you gotta go—"

Indecision clogs my mind again. Leaving Drew and the dog seems callous, and I need to find someone to fix *Sassy*.

Maybe I can trust Drew . . . After all, the stray trusts him. I always put stock in how animals react to humans. *Even the street rats would've run from Connor.*

I swallow. "It's okay. I'll come. Lead the way."

CHAPTER 3

"Can you hold the leash?" Drew passes the belt to me without waiting for an answer. He unwinds the T-shirt from around his hand and pulls it on.

Walking beside him, Drew's height surprises me. At five feet ten, I'm normally close in height to most men, but he has at least another five inches on me.

A while ago, I learned that if I ask lots of questions, people don't have the chance to ask questions back—anything to avoid talking about myself or my family. "How'd you get involved at the shelter?"

"I've seen too much not to get involved. The locals hate the strays because they affect tourism. Some dogs are captured and killed and fed to the cattle. Others are shot. They chuck their carcasses into the local landfill. The cyclone went through here while I was snowboarding with Brett in Colorado last year. The animal shelters became desperate for volunteers, and there was this rumor that the Samoan government planned to fix the problem by canning dog meat and exporting it as pet food."

"That's horrible." People can be so cruel and vicious. "Did they actually do it?" The banana trees lining the road don't provide much shade and I swipe the sweat beads from my forehead.

"Not yet. But I'm taking a break from vet school, so I thought I could offer some help."

"Does Brett volunteer, too?"

"No. He's more interested in the inside of bars and checking out women on the beach." Drew winces. "Sorry, shouldn't have said that." He pauses, contemplating me.

A lazy afternoon breeze lifts my hair, fluttering it behind me. Drew's eyes widen as he takes me in.

I stare at our feet, letting my hair act as a curtain. "Have you known Brett long?"

"All my life." Drew drops another chip. "When he heard I was going overseas, he tagged along. Bit of a lost cause."

"What do you mean?"

"Nothing, really." He scuffs up dust with his bare feet. His gaze slides back to mine, heavy with unspoken words. He shoves his free hand into the pocket of his khaki shorts. "What about you? Why are you in Samoa?"

Pricks of shock scatter all over my skin. *I need to develop my lying skills.* "The usual traveling stuff. I used to teach sailing." My teeth grab my lower lip. I search for a way to change the subject. "I just realized . . . I left my flip-flops in the café."

He scrutinizes me—my tank top suddenly feels too tight and my shorts too short. "Public service. A local will have shoes today, thanks to you. Unless a tourist nicks them first."

The road narrows, and the banana trees fatten and tower like shade umbrellas. Drew veers to the left, toward a narrow footpath. "It's this way. Give the dog some room, in case she feels cornered." Drew moves lithely over fallen branches and rocks, checking back now and again. When the path opens into a field, he stops.

"That's the clinic." He points across the sun-scorched grass at a concrete structure with a tin-sheet roof. Around the building are several caged areas, and I hear the occasional bark.

I squint into the glare at the pot-holed road leading to the clinic and try to imagine the cyclone hitting. "Sienna might stop by. She volunteers, too. She got me some shifts in the bar at the beach resort where she works."

"The vet work isn't well-paid, then?"

"Unpaid. It's volunteer stuff as I'm not qualified yet. The resort's okay though. They provide basic shared accommodation—no TV or private bathrooms—but right on the beach, and I use the days off to come here or if there's emergency re-building work at the village nearby."

"You're re-building a *village*?"

"That sounded like I was bragging. Just helping, following the cyclone. There are loads of us."

A cluster of dogs from the shelter howl. Our stray growls then tugs at the belt, dragging Drew. A man comes out of the clinic as we approach.

"Talofa," he shouts. He's somewhere in his late forties, although his receding hairline might make him appear older. Drew responds in Samoan, saying a word that sounds like "Oh-ah-my-oh-eh."

"Brought us another one, son. I thought y'all had finished your shift?" I can tell by his accent that he's from Texas.

"She was getting herself into trouble," Drew replies. "And this is Emily. She helped me. Emily, this is Vic Hawkins, the resident vet."

Vic dips his chin at me and scans the dog's body. He retrieves a treat from the pocket of his white doctor coat. The dog gobbles it from his palm and sniffs the pocket for more.

"Sure is good to meet you, Emily," Vic says. "Call me Vic."

Drew snorts. "You told me to call you sir the first time we met."

Vic regards Drew warmly and slaps him on the back

before going indoors. The stray traipses behind him. Drew stands aside to let me pass through the narrow door, but I still somehow brush his chest with my arm. My breath grips.

Inside, two long stainless-steel tables fill the cramped room. Surgical equipment and colored plastic containers, labeled syringes, swabs, or gloves clutter the space. The shelves on the walls are stacked with cardboard boxes. Dust cakes the windows, making it necessary for the lights to be on.

"Be my assistant, Drew? Just to restrain her."

"Sure." Drew's gaze flicks to me under arched eyebrows. "Do you mind waiting? I'll take you back to the harbor after this."

"Do what you need to do. I'm fine."

"Take a load off." Drew points to a rickety wooden chair in the corner, then opens a small fridge on the opposite side of the room. When he nears to pass me a bottle of chilled water, our smiles match, as if we're sharing a secret.

Vic lifts the dog onto one of the examining tables and whips a muzzle onto her. They work together to flip the dog onto her side. Drew places his elbow on the dog's neck, hooking a hand through the front legs. His body hovers across the middle of the dog while his other hand clasps the back legs.

The more time I spend with Drew, the more I like him. He's interesting. Easy to talk to. And without even a smidge of sleaze about him. The guys I met back home in high school—before Connor—seemed seedy or defensive, or as if they were saying what they believed I wanted to hear. Even the older ones I met while crewing were the same way. Being very clear about the message I sent the crews over the years was important—*pretend I'm just a buddy*. In the end, they decided I was shy, and probably gay—why else wouldn't I be interested in any of them? But they respected my sailing ability enough to let me remain in the shadows

19

and after Connor came onto the scene, they backed right off.

Drew is new territory, though. I don't feel like he's a circling shark. And I don't have the desire to be invisible to him.

In the corner of the clinic is a corkboard pinned with photos of animals and pencil sketches of dogs. The drawings catch the emotions of each dog—one's excited, another's bored, another's hopeful, possibly of some morsel. Many of them are half-starved bags of bones, some missing an eye or a leg. The strays. They look broken. *As I am.*

"Do you like Drew's drawings?" Vic asks. He snaps off his white plastic gloves, the procedure over.

"They're brilliant." I move closer to inspect them. "You captured the expressions so accurately, Drew."

Drew grabs the back of his neck and strokes the dog. He contemplates me, and one corner of his mouth lifts into an adorable half-smile. I'm surprised to see shyness there. It hits me that the pull I'm feeling toward him . . . he's feeling it, too.

The hot breeze coming in through the door suddenly makes the room too warm, too small, and my palms dampen. *Would he be attracted to me if he knew why I'm on the run?*

"Y'all can put the ol' girl in a cage now, Drew."

Drew does as he's asked, and I listen to him chat with the dogs outside. The cage gate shatters shut as a car scrunches to a halt.

"Vic! Emergency." A girl about Drew's age with a pixie-cute face, stylish, short dark hair, and a perfect elfin body to match rushes through the doorway carrying a white mongrel caked in blood.

"You're an injured dog magnet, Sienna," Vic says. He's already donning a clean pair of gloves and disinfecting the table. Sienna puts the half-conscious animal on its side. Her white sundress is bloody and dirty. "This is serious."

Sienna glances up as Drew enters the room. "Hey, Drew."

"Hey." Drew's gaze stays on me.

Sienna inspects me. Her pale, lightly freckled skin flushes and her green eyes sparkle—the type of green that's reflected from rainbows. "Hello. Are you a new volunteer?" she asks.

I switch on a bright smile. "Not officially. Just happened to be there to help." She's staring at me way too hard. I suddenly realize I must be crazy. My story could be head-lining on the news. Any one of these people could recognize me.

Vic suddenly shouts instructions to Sienna and Drew about fetching a few things from the storeroom. They race outside. Vic's cleaned up the wound, and it's clear the dog is missing half its skull. "Emily," he says, without looking up, "the box on the third shelf, marked spares . . . fetch it down now."

Caught up in the emergency, I will myself to remain calm. I drag the chair across to the shelves, locate the box he asked for, and mount the chair. When I pull the box off the shelf, it's unbelievably heavy. I grunt. With a cracking sound, the chair collapses beneath me. Drew breaks my fall. His arms envelop me, the heat of him pressing against my back. But only for a moment. In one smooth movement, Drew yanks the box from my hands, hauls it onto the table, and kneels on the floor as if he's dropped something.

"Sienna's fainted," Drew says from the floor. "Hit her head. Big gash."

"Emily, fetch Drew a compress." Vic points behind him. "Green plastic box."

I settle on the other side of Sienna, tear the packaging open, and give the compress to Drew. He applies pressure to a wound on Sienna's temple. I work to straighten Sienna's waif-like body, untie my hoodie, and fold it into a pillow, hoping no one notices the hard lump of cash. I move to Sien-na's feet and lift them, remembering the steps I learned in my marine medical course I took before I started teaching sailing.

Sienna stirs and attempts to sit.

"You fainted and banged your head," Drew says. "You'll be fine but lie still."

I keep Sienna's legs raised and catch Drew's stare. His apologetic expression silently asks if I'm okay. I smile in response, and it's as if there's a bridge being built between us. I've never had such subtle body language communication with anyone before. It feels too intense.

The sound of another car pulling up has Vic exclaiming, "What the hell?"

I recognize Brett when he strolls into the clinic. "Doesn't look good, doc."

"Not now, eh, Brett? Drew's down there." Vic points with an elbow.

Brett peers over the table. When he sees me, his brows lift, then pinch into a frown. "Hello, Gotta Go Girl." Brett examines Drew, his face loaded with questions, then he grunts, "Sienna. Drew."

"Hey, Brett," Sienna and Drew answer in unison.

"No one told me there was a party happening here." His grin sweeps the room, but everyone ignores him.

"I'm sorry," Sienna whispers. "God. I don't know what happened."

"Can't stomach the sight of blood?" Drew asks.

She shivers. "I thought I could see the dog's brain."

"You need to go to the hospital," Drew says. "Judging by the gash on your head, you should get checked out."

"Head injury. Brett, take Sienna to the hospital," Vic orders. "And bless your fluffy soul."

Brett assumes Vic's joking, but after scanning the three of us on the floor, he rolls his eyes. "Jeez, I donated money so I wouldn't need to work here. Remember?"

"And I was fixin' to have an already late lunch," Vic adds. "But can you all get out now? I'm conducting surgery here."

I grab my hoodie and tie it around my waist, wondering if Drew will go to the hospital with Sienna.

Vic doesn't look away from the dog when he says, "Thanks, Emily. Sure could do with someone like you round here. Level-headed in an emergency."

I stop myself telling him that solo sailors must remain calm, no matter what gets thrown at them.

Outside, Drew shuts the car door on Sienna. "Thanks, mate," he murmurs to Brett. "I owe you. I need to feed the dogs because Vic can't, and I should walk Emily back."

"S'okay. There's this hot nurse I met before. Said she'd come for a drink later, so guess I'll be early. Save her the agony of waiting to see me again."

Before Brett climbs into the driver's seat, his dark gaze seeks me out. He wiggles his eyebrows suggestively then winks. Drew's already distributing dry kibble into the cages and filling water bowls when Brett drives away.

"Be with you in a minute," Drew hollers. He chats with the dogs, bending to respond to a whine or to stroke a deliriously happy mongrel. "Thanks for your help today. Are you training to be a doctor?"

I smirk. "In another lifetime."

"Where are you staying?"

A sudden image of *Sassy* watching the sunset alone casts a shadow over my mood. "Let's not do the backpacker conversation. You must have asked that a hundred times since you got here." I fiddle with the knot of my hoodie and move away from the cages.

Drew's suddenly by my side again. My insides tickle.

He runs his fingers through his hair, peers down at me. "I'm only asking where you're staying so I know where we're going. I'm not a stalker . . ."

I jerk to meet Drew's steel-blue eyes, then leave myself

trapped there a moment longer, groping for the right words. "I'm not very trusting, am I?" We walk back toward the banana trees. "Sorry. It comes from traveling alone."

"Guess that makes sense. Look what happened to you today. You met a crazed stray dog and at least two psychos." Drew bumps shoulders with me, and I'm utterly aware of his breath on my cheek. All I can focus on is how to make him do that again, somehow, anyhow, right now. I don't want to say goodbye.

What happened to my vow to stay clear of men? *I'm so weak, like my mom.*

"Reckon you're pretty good at looking after yourself," Drew adds, breaking the silence.

I reprimand myself for letting him turn me into Play-Doh. I've forgotten *Sassy*. The windvane. My goal to reach Australia. My crime. *How's that looking after myself?*

The word *murderer* sidles into my brain and dwells there like a flickering candle.

CHAPTER 4

"Would you like to get something to eat?" Drew asks as the harbor comes into view.

"I don't think so," I almost snap. "I've gotta go. It's nearly dark." My hair falls across my face. I wonder if this is the right time to ask about the boat guy. I need to introduce *Sassy* carefully, without alerting him to the fact that I'm not a traveler named Emily.

"Can I at least walk you to your hotel or hostel or—?"

"Only if you've got an hour. I'm a few bays across from here."

"Heard of a thing called a taxi in that there place Cali-forn-i-a? Come on, after this afternoon's drama, I feel like treating myself . . . and you." He lifts a finger to push my hair behind my ear so he can see my face better. It seems presumptuous, but his smile is kind, his words warm. And his light touch has punctured something inside me. Maybe because I've been alone for two months, I don't want to leave. I'm not ready to be lonely again.

I contemplate the cafés along the harbor. They've turned on their welcoming lights. Music and spicy aromas waft in the warm evening air and the thought of tinned or freeze-

dried food on *Sassy* weakens my will further. *I'm starving.*
"Okay. A *quick* bite."

Drew offers me his hand. I hesitate. He curls his fingers
softly around mine, making my insides turn into slippery
melted butter. A longing to lean against him, to be held,
surprises me. Perhaps it's not a weird reaction—I've been
hungering for human contact for weeks, especially on the
days when the loneliness made me feel as if I was the last
person left on Earth. I'd feel the same way, no matter who I
got talking to. Plus, there's something about sharing an experience like this afternoon that's bonded us.

"There's a great restaurant up here," he says.

I stop walking.

Sitting at a table in a restaurant with a man … with Drew?
And what if I'm recognized?

Drew fakes exasperation and there's that rich, full-bellied
laughter again. "What now?" When he releases my hand, I
wish he hadn't.

"I'm not that hungry," I lie. "How about takeout fish and
chips? Somewhere less crowded?"

"Trying to get me alone, are you?"

My blush matches the cherry-tinted sunset.

"Okay, but we can do better than fish and chips." Drew
picks up the pace. "Something more Samoan."

I inspect the array of cafés along the harbor. "Like
what?"

"You'll have to *trust* me." He nudges my arm. "This place I
know. They cook everything in a central umu. I prefer to eat
what the locals do, otherwise I may as well never leave
Australia."

I lengthen my stride to keep up. "What's an umu?"

"An open fire. They make food your taste buds will
worship you for. Hey, you do know how to use a knife and
fork? We don't want a repeat of this afternoon's plate lick-
ing." We laugh aloud. "So why were you so starved?"

Eyes lowered, an unstoppable grin leaps to my lips. "What are you saying? I always eat like that."

Drew cracks up, and I give myself a metaphorical pat on the back.

He stops at a restaurant surrounded with flame torches. It has a takeout order window. "I'd recommend the lu'au. It's taro with coconut cream and onions. Sounds nothing special, but once you eat it, you'll never forget it."

I frown at the menu written on a blackboard to the side. I have no clue what most of it is. "I'll try that then."

"Do you want some kava? It's a local drink, but not very strong."

"I don't really drink alcohol." I don't explain that from what I've seen, it changes people—it changes stockbrokers into monsters.

A Samoan man wearing a colorful tropical shirt takes our order. I turn away to hide my face. When Drew's done, he leans against the counter, facing me, his arms crossed.

"How much do I owe you?" I ask.

"Accept it as a thank you for helping me today." Drew's gaze rummages inside my eyes as he speaks. *Thank goodness it's dusk.*

I return to my question-asking technique. "So, will Brett come for you later?"

"Are you interested in Brett?" Drew chuckles, but there's an edge to it, like when you make yourself laugh at a joke that offends you.

"No! Why would you think that?"

"You ask about him a lot. And he can be quite . . . enigmatic."

The pit of my belly whorls with nerves, and I try to figure out how to change the conversation to the English boat guy.

"You don't do small talk, do you?" he asks after an awkward silence. "Let's do the opposite of small talk then. A deep and meaningful conversation." He contemplates my face like an artist noticing every detail. "How's this? *My* story is I'm on the run. What's yours?"

He must be freaking joking.

I stiffen like a peg doll. "Something like that."

He smirks. "What? You're a twenty-four-year-old bloke who ran away from home?"

I actually giggle.

"Guess you can't really run away from home when you're my age, but I've dropped out for a while—family issues." He scans the length of the horizon. "My father wants me to take over the family business. One of the many downsides of being an only child. And he can be a bit of a bully when it comes to getting his way and controlling my life. I'm surprised he hasn't sent some heavies to drag me home. Hey, are *you* his spy?" His tongue is literally in his cheek, and his eyes resemble twin Sirius stars.

I want to respond with something snappy, but nothing comes. Instead, I ask, "What's so bad about taking over the family business?"

He's doing that searching my face thing again. "I'm amazed I told you that. I've been traveling for a year and never once mentioned it."

Somehow thrilled, I smother a smile. "I can't see you in a suit," I tease, surprising myself.

"'Cos I'm standing here looking like an awesome hunk of surfer dude?" He bumps shoulders with me, and my heart curls at the edges and flutters. "Cheeky, aren't you?"

"My father and Connor used to call me sassy." The words slip out of my brain and out of my mouth before I can stop them. Yet, it's been such a long time since I've been even close to acting high-spirited. Connor had seen to that.

"Used to?" Drew asks.

Shit. The sun squints on the horizon. I close my eyes, pretending it's too bright. When I open them, I make my hand into a visor. "My father died. Recently. I'd rather not talk about him."

A snapshot of a memory returns—of my mother's voice telling me over the phone that my father had been in a car accident, of feeling relieved he was dead, of hating myself for being relieved. But it meant my father couldn't take my mother on the six-month trip he'd planned on *Sassy Jam*. I had been sure one or both would not return. Either he'd fall overboard while drunk or knock my mother overboard during a fight.

"I'm sorry." Drew hands me some plastic forks and napkins. "Is that why you're traveling for a while?"

"I needed to get away. After he died . . ." My tongue doesn't trip over the lies this time.

Silence simmers. New understanding nudges across Drew's features.

"I get it," he whispers. "My mom died when I was four-teen. We cope in the only way we know how." It's his turn to stare into space. His grief makes him seem more imperfect, less Adonis-like. More like me. "My mother was hot on eating and drinking as the locals do when we traveled. 'Authentic' was her favorite word."

The guy in the Hawaiian shirt passes out our food. Drew takes it, and we walk toward the harbor wall. "Lu'au is very *authentic*." He sniffs inside the brown bag, checking our order. "So, when did you arrive in Samoa?"

"Just today actually. What about you and Brett?"

"Got here a little over a month ago. Started in New York a year ago. Been bungee jumping in Ohio, white-water rafting in Indiana, then drove to Colorado for the heli-snowboard-ing. New York chewed up most of my savings, so I've been working my way around. But it's good to get work. You meet people. It's all new experiences—living *authentically* with the locals."

"Sounds admirable, especially considering some cultures eat bugs. How do you know Brett?"

Drew chuckles and pretends to drop the bag of food. "There you go, again. Brett, Brett, Brett…"

I giggle, sounding identical to Emily. "I only want to know how you met."

"A guy could get jealous, you know." Some other emotion spoils his smile. "He's a bit of a party nut, so if you're keen on him, I hope you're into partying hard."

"He's too sleazy," I say to assure Drew of my lack of interest. "It's exhausting just being in the same space. What was that about the donation to Vic though?"

"Brett talked his parents into donating to the shelter to avoid volunteering. They're loaded. Made him feel less guilty. So, the man you're so interested in is totally work-shy."

"I'm *not* interested in him." Drew inspects me. Embarrassed, I blurt, "You didn't answer my question. About not wanting to work for your dad."

Drew's smile snags. A collage of emotion rifles across his face. "Where do I start? I can't connect with finance and IT. It doesn't excite me. My dad and I don't get on. I'd rather do something with animals or something more artistic. I'm actually a complete coward and ran away from the problem until I decide what to do."

When we reach the harbor wall, we sit with the brown bag between us, our legs dangling over the sloshing water. I decide it's a good time to broach the subject of getting *Sassy* fixed.

"Do you have a phone?" I could borrow it to search for some boatyards.

"Sorry, no. It broke when I was snowboarding. I landed on it after attempting a jump, and I didn't exactly have the funds to buy a new one. Did you need to call someone?"

"No. No big deal." I give the sleeve of my hoodie several twists, making a material snake. Drew's been in Samoa for over a month and has been traveling before then. He probably hasn't seen a news bulletin in weeks. There's no TV at his resort. And he knows a lot about the island. It feels as if I can trust him. "I thought your dad had a successful business. Wouldn't he send you money if you needed it?"

Drew flexes his jaw, frowns. "Do you need money?'

"No, no. Not for me. For you. You could get a new phone."

"My dad and I are not exactly on speaking terms. He's angry I left, not just vet school but the continent. We argued the day before, and I took off with a backpack and the meager funds in my account. All with Brett in tow. To be honest, I'd been sponging. I was studying, but I could've broken ties and refused my father's funding. I was ashamed of myself. It's hard not to take the easy route when it's offered. But then he used that and a couple of other things to blackmail me—said I had to give the family business two years before deciding it wasn't for me. Apparently, my grandfather is turning in his grave, thanks to me."

He'd left his home with as much notice as I had.

I take in a deep breath. "Okay. The truth is I solo sailed to Samoa."

"From America?" His laugh is more of a bark. He sits back, looking impressed.

I hope he's not making connections with a news story he's seen in a bar or on an international flight. "You said you knew someone who knows about boats. My self-steering mechanism is broken, I need diesel, new lifelines—"

"*Jeez.* When did you set out? What sort of boat are you on?"

"About two months ago. And she's a thirty-four-foot sailboat, set up for a solo sailor. My dad was into sailing." *There I go again, mentioning Dad.* "I inherited his boat. My mom said I learned to walk on a catamaran the summer we sailed up and down the California coast for six weeks. Apparently, I

31

walked on the boat, but went back to crawling when on land, like the boat seemed safer to me."

"I've heard about a few people solo sailing the world. It must take so much courage." His smiling gaze reaches in and loops its magic inside me.

"I'm not circumnavigating the globe though, simply going to Australia." I don't tell him how my uncle and brother live there and that my mother followed them after my dad died. And that Uncle Brody is a lawyer. I need his help now.

"No kidding. Where in Australia?"

"Queensland."

"You don't want to go there. Full of crocodiles and killer snakes." We laugh, both running our fingers through our hair. "And yeah, I know a guy who can help you fix your boat. What's it like, being at sea alone?"

"The ocean resembles ink at night with ruffles of white lace. The sky darkens and merges with it. It's as if gravity stops working. When I'm all alone out there, I'm a pinpoint on a cosmic map, floating somewhere on the line between the ocean and the sky."

"Weren't you afraid?"

"At first." I remember how a rising unease would tighten my throat. "But I found ways to make myself feel safer. I tied a Jesus line to the back of the boat as an extra precaution, and that helped."

"What's a Jesus line?"

"A towrope. It acts as a 'last chance' grab rope if you fall overboard. Before I did that, I had nightmares about the boat sailing unmanned without me."

"What was the hardest part?" Drew's expression is both baffled and intrigued.

I don't know where to start. The loneliness. The storms I thought I wouldn't survive, the shark that circled me for days. The lack of fresh food. "The doldrums," I say eventually. "I was stuck there for weeks. No wind, which meant I didn't move an inch. No diesel for the motor. No paddles. I'd lost them both."

"Wow. You're a lot braver than me." His expression brims with admiration. "You must've had a lot of time for thinking," Drew says, "about life and the future. Did you come up with any epiphanies?"

"Yes. Even though the doldrums are a beautiful part of the world, I realized I need goals. I can't sit around all day."

I longed for evidence that I wasn't the only person left on Earth. I'd searched for anything—a discarded soda can, some floating plant debris—just to give me hope. On one of the days, I thought I saw three white blossoms floating on the gray ocean. I jumped on the roof, expecting to see land, but the fog was too thick. I sniffed for grass and earth and tree sap. But all there was, was salt. When I looked for the blossoms again, they were no longer there. With them, went my hope.

"Lolling alone in a people-less world on the far side of the sunset might seem appealing, but it had felt as if I was half-alive."

Now that most of the truth is on the table, our exchange becomes easier and winds on, a never-ending pathway. Drew listens to me talk about *Sassy*, the storms, the loneliness, the food, and the near-death experiences. Our words and laughter hum in the sultry night air. We weave connections between and around us, the conversation a spinning cocoon that binds us closer.

Or entraps.

CHAPTER 5

Drew insists on putting me in a taxi back to Valusu Bay. It's late and dark and not a safe walk. We wait on the side of the road. I am lost for words, knowing I'll probably never see him again.

A beat-up car pulls to the curb. There's no evidence of a taxi sign, and inside, there's no meter. Drew leans into the passenger window and tells the driver the destination, then negotiates a fixed price.

"How do you know he's a taxi?" I ask when Drew straightens. This could be a trick.

"The number plates start with a T."

I can't stop feeling suspicious, but at the same time, I thrill in his nearness, his height, how broad he is compared to me. Maybe Connor didn't damage me completely.

At the thought of saying goodbye, possibly forever, my brain gets stage fright. Drew opens the taxi door, and I climb in. Before I can turn to wave, he squishes in beside me.

"Scoot over," he says.

I'm squashed against a huge box that's also in the backseat.

"*Hey.*" My pulse spikes. *Is he kidnapping me? Making an arrest?*

"I can't let some strange bloke take you off into the night," Drew says. "Don't worry. I'll return you to your boat and leave you in peace."

His bare leg presses against mine. Our arms are dusty and tacky against each other. I grab at the box and the seat in front to rein in the drowning sensation. I haven't sat this close to a man other than Connor before, and not one that has my heart torpedoing around my ribcage.

"So, this English boat guy . . ." My voice comes out different, breathy.

"He lives a few miles up from Lalomanu Beach and the Coconut Palm Beach Resort—you know, the place where I work? When you're ready, come down. It's much prettier than this side of the island, too. The beaches are white, and there are swimming coves, waterfalls, snorkeling. I'll introduce you then. He teaches surfing at the resort, and he's sailed the world. I don't have his number on me now."

"Thanks, Drew." My tongue curls around his name for the first time; it's as if there's static electricity in my mouth.

"S'okay. What are friends for?" He holds my gaze, his face so close our breaths swirl together. For a moment, I suspect he wants to kiss me. *This can't happen. I'm on the run. I'm a bad person. Someday they'll catch up with me, and I'll be in prison for the rest of my life.*

"What's with the box?" I turn to the box, push at it to give us more space, but it doesn't budge.

"Driver's getting two jobs in one. He'll deliver it during a fare. A kind of taxi-postal service." Drew rubs his hands up and down his thighs before he lets them rest on his knees.

My thumb worries at a rough fingernail, flicks the zip on my hoodie. "Hope the dinghy's still there." When he gives me a puzzled look, I add, "My boat's anchored a few hundred meters offshore. I paddled in." My voice sounds different, as if there's not enough air in the taxi.

Apart from pointing out some historical buildings, Drew remains silent. I try to breathe normally. I take in how he smells both like limes and . . . it can only be described as *male*. When the taxi stops, the headlights reflect off the white-painted boulders lining the road. Drew holds the door open for me. I thrust some money at him.

"Tala not dollars. You need to change your cash." He asks the driver to wait, then follows me across the rocks until we spot the orange dinghy. "You're going to paddle out to sea in the dark?" he asks, already knowing the answer.

"I have a flashlight." I unzip an invisible pocket in the dinghy and flick on the extra-bright fluorescent light.

He takes it and shines it on the water, but the beam doesn't reach *Sassy*.

"I'll find her. Don't worry. I've navigated from California to Samoa, so I'll manage a few hundred meters." I chuck the hoodie into the dinghy. "Make yourself useful and help me push it into the water?" I put my sailing head on—the responsible one, the one that doesn't pine for his company. We push the dinghy until it's at the water's edge.

"Bet you're actually staying in one of those houses back there," Drew teases.

I straighten and laugh freely, savoring the last of our banter. His eyes widen as he watches me. I move to playfully punch his arm, but quick as a flash, he catches my hand, threads his fingers through mine, and steps in so close I hear his sharp inhale.

"I liked spending time with you today," he murmurs near my ear, his voice throaty.

All the jumpiness inside me is replaced by a wafting sensation of lightness drifting through my veins. Not trusting myself to speak, I lift my face and let my eyes answer, "me too." I half-smile. His expression is soft and caressing and a split-second later, his lips graze my cheek.

Rather than push him away as I should, I pause, take in how exquisite tremors whisk through my body. His mouth moves to brush my lips, barely touching, more of a question from his lips to mine.

"'Night," he manages, husky.

I totter backward. "'Night." The word comes out as more of a whispered 'i' sound.

Drew surrenders my hand and we shove at the dinghy. He follows me into the shallows, and we charge deeper into the water, propelling it into the break. I jump in and our fingertips touch. It feels like an important moment in time. The seconds elongate as I glance from his fingers to his face, wanting him to know, in case we never see each other again, that I wasn't shocked by his kiss, more astounded by the way he woke my body from the dead.

CHAPTER 6

Intense sunlight brightens my eyelids, elbowing me awake. I roll over to check the time. Ten-thirty. I slept nine straight hours. During the crossing, I'd had to wake every twenty minutes to do safety checks and rarely got more than four hours of sleep a day.

The porthole frames the spot where Drew kissed me good night on the beach last night. Connor's kisses, the only man I'd ever slept with, were always passionate and demanding, seeming to want to possess me—and that was when he was in a good mood. I'd had to resist the impulse to pull back from him. But Drew's kiss only left me wanting more. Drew's was the fairy-tale kiss I'd wondered about when I was a little girl, before my father changed and my parent's marriage was doomed. Before Connor.

I didn't think it possible to miss someone I'd spent thirteen hours with. After being alone at sea for two months, it is comparable to being let out of prison for one day, having the best day ever, then being locked up again. Books written by sailors describe the first night away from port as the hardest —we must adjust to the solo sailor's life of loneliness. But I wonder if this sensation is solo sailor syndrome or Drew sickness.

I try to imagine what Drew's doing right then in Lalomanu. Thoughts of him make me calm and soft inside. But as I examine the map to set a course for his resort, I'm gripped by doubt. I misjudged Connor once, what if I'm doing it again with Drew? Drew didn't mention this boat guy's name or any real details. He could be luring me there, only to take me to bed. With men, what you see on the outside isn't what's on the inside. And I'm on the run from the law. I can't hang around just because of some fairy-tale kiss. Already Drew has me making dubious choices.

Drew can't happen.

Don't ever rely on anyone but yourself. That's what my older brother had said before he left for Australia seven years ago. He couldn't stand our parents fighting, either. He had abandoned his UCLA plans and moved to Queensland to work in Uncle Brody's side business—he ran a boatyard when he wasn't working as a lawyer. Before Finn emigrated, life had been about balancing on a precarious raft but at least he was there beside me. After he left, the raft broke apart. The rowing between our parents went from heated arguments to hitting.

Whenever a fight started, I would hide in my room. I'd lose myself in sailing posters while earbuds blasted music into my skull to drown out the slapping and crying. Hugging a pillow, I rocked back and forth, hating myself because I was a copy of my mom—I let the fighting happen and never did anything to stop it. My mother never spoke of the incidents. The one time I brought it up, she became angry and refused to drive me to the sailing club. She said all couples argue and that she banged her cheek on the door frame when she got upset and ran from the bedroom. What was I meant to do? As my father always said, I was 'just a girl.'

I had believed Connor Stratton was my life raft. Though I

was only eighteen, I grabbed what he offered—a fast route out of home, and what I thought was love—with both hands. He was ten years my senior, and he seemed so together. A successful stockbroker and from a respectable family. Out of the frying pan and into the fire.

I reach for the kettle and push my mind to think about something else. Because this 'just a girl' survived the Pacific, even though my father hadn't ever allowed me to solo sail *Sassy. I'll survive the rest of the way to Australia, too.*

Today's plan. First, find an internet café to locate boat repair yards.

Second, forget Drew.

HAVING TIED the dinghy to the palm tree again, I scuff at the dusty road to kick a hole in the hush. The day is stifling and still and dark cumulonimbus clouds gather. A flock of parrots break away from the wild hibiscus shrubs and into a sky where shafts of sun bully their way through gaps in the cloud. I lift my face to watch the parrots circle and re-group, then stick my tongue out to catch tiny splinters of rain.

I avoid the fish café, avoid the harbor wall and the lu'au restaurant, avoid the area where we waited for a taxi. A chalkboard on the sidewalk advertises currency exchange services. The bank teller speaks English and offers me a tourist map but can't help with finding a boatyard. Instead, she gives me directions to the internet café around the corner.

With its green Formica tables and sun-bleached blue plastic chairs, the café has a western air to it. Backpackers both hang out and work behind the counter while strains of *Drake* pour out of an old-fashioned radio. I buy coconut juice and banana bread from a girl with five piercings in one ear.

The girl gives me the password and instructs me to choose a computer from the row against the sidewall.

The first thing I learn is the date. August 13th. It's as if I've lost two months of my life.

Several boatyard searches later, I come up with nothing except descriptions and photos of the harbor. Once a boatyard name surfaces, but without an address or phone number. It's possible Western Samoa's list of services hasn't been inputted into cyberspace yet.

The staff can't help, either. When I ask their advice, it's clear they're travelers, too. I could search the harbor again or sail to another more populated island where I'll more readily find what *Sassy* needs. I punch in Google maps and my current location. The screen shoots up the twin islands of Western Samoa as well as American Samoa, Fiji, and Tonga. But instead of checking distances to bigger islands, I guide the cursor to zoom into the southeast side of Samoa to locate Lalomanu Beach, click in further to the Coconut Palm Beach Resort. Even thinking about Drew makes my insides pleasantly pull.

The idea of downloading my emails crawls into my brain. My mom might've sent a message or I could send her one. But the police are probably monitoring our accounts and can find out where I accessed my email. I whizz the yacht pendant on my necklace up and down. My mother had given it to me after dad's funeral four months ago as a parting gift before she left for Australia. She had her own bad memories to escape. My gut squeezes and twists, the feeling of missing my family momentarily distracts me. The chain breaks. Pushing back tears, I pocket the pieces in my cut-off denim shorts.

I type my name into Google. More listings than I can believe pop onto the screen. My heart jackhammers in my chest. *Channel Seven. ABC News. NBC.* My fingers tremble over the mouse, moving it to a *CNN* link dated yesterday. A massive picture of me holding up a sailing trophy from a competition pops open.

Missing. Shae Love sighted near Hawaii!
The police search across all states, now in its ninth week, has come to a dead end. Initial evidence suggested Miss Love (23) was hiding on the family sailboat—

"Is that you?"

I jerk toward the girl with five earrings as she looks over my shoulder at the screen. Fear blasts through my veins like shrapnel from a bomb blast. I will myself to smile, click off the page, and stand.

"Twin sister," I say. "She won this big sailing competition. Wish it *was* me."

"I hear ya, girlfriend." The girl blows a bubble with her gum and raises a fist for me to bump.

My chest chugs. We bump fists. I clear my search history and walk out the café and into a cramped dress shop where I can be anonymous.

The police know I'm on Sassy. It's only a matter of time.

Even though I knew they'd be looking for me, it all seems in-my-face real now. Maybe I should turn myself in. I've proved I can solo sail, despite my dad once scoffing at the possibility. Proved I can survive everything the Pacific can throw at me. I've lived my dream. But I'm in Samoa. I don't know their legal system. It's not American Samoa. I recall the footage of inhumane prisons in Thailand after a teenage girl was jailed for life for drug trafficking. What if prisons are similar in Western Samoa? Fear clutches at me. It'll be safer to get to Australia and Uncle Brody. He'll know what to do. He'll defend me. *Stick to the original plan.*

Despite the lightning out to sea, I search for a boatyard on the streets farther from the center, walking until my spare flip-flops rub a blister into my foot, and my tongue sticks to the roof of my mouth. Conceivably the boatyards aren't near the main harbor. I head inland, but it's soon obvious I must sail to a bigger island.

AFTER HAULING MYSELF ABOARD *SASSY*, my feet scrunch a large piece of paper in the middle of the cockpit, weighed down by a green coconut. A badly spelled message is scrawled in navy ink.

Boat repare man is George. Number is 41 555. At Saleapaga Beach 6 mils from Coconut Palm Rasort. Him sort everyting.

My first thought is a warm one—Drew hadn't forgotten me. A second thought is that he sent this note via messenger, unless he never graduated from second grade. Somehow the messenger, the note, Drew's wanting to help all seem to tell me to trust him. And to stay.

The idea of seeing Drew drives a thrill ride straight through me. Maybe after being lonely for so long, I simply crave company and laughter. But do I go to him or to Fiji to get the windvane fixed? Doing it here would be quicker and safer and save me sailing long days to Fiji without the windvane. *Crap.* I should've checked for boat repairs in Fiji. What if they're not listed online, either? And someone could recognize me on any island. It's best to stay on a less populated one.

I won't let anything develop between me and Drew. *Friends only.*

Given the windvane is broken, I decide to set sail at first light.

HALF AN HOUR LATER, I notice some locals in a dinghy heading toward me. I take advantage of the fading light and head farther out to sea to anchor for the night. After seeing the *CNN* story earlier, I'm extra jumpy about being recognized.

That evening, thunder clouds filled with lilac sit heavily on the horizon. It's other-worldly. The sun slinks below the horizon, signaling the seagulls to leave me for their nests. The Earth becomes ancient and lifeless. I wander from the silent cabin to the cockpit, bringing in dry clothes from the lines before it rains. The night is dead calm. I'm reminded of the lull before the storm.

At some point, I jump awake in my bunk, heart thrusting against bone at the sound of police sirens and someone telling me that murder carries a life sentence and laughing at my version of the truth. Fighting panic is like gift-wrapping a porcupine. Every time I push down and cover over the feeling, a spike of alarm pokes through, refusing to be papered down.

"Where do I hide?" The words swell inside the silent cabin.

I hold my breath to listen. The wind wails, an unleashed wild animal raging, circling, prodding, and waiting for the right moment to attack. The ocean lashes against the portholes. The clock behind me indicates it's midnight. The familiar roar of the Pacific blasts, resembling a blaring television inside the cabin. I stow the bunk as the back of the boat rises—a vast wave tilts us forward. I grip the handholds, stand astride. We're almost vertical. It's the same as a carnival ride where the room tips and the floor becomes the wall. My stomach lurches. *We could pitch-pole into the trough.* I didn't realize how far out to sea I anchored, and I had been so preoccupied with Drew's note that the possibility of a tropical storm hadn't crossed my mind. He's turned me to Play-Doh again.

CHAPTER 7

The portholes snapshot a wall of water on both sides before *Sassy* jerks and judders into the trough, but the wave cradles us and instead of cartwheeling to a crushing end, we level out and lurch up the other side. My father once said fear freezes the brain and stops decisive action that can save your life. I must knock it out of me, like it's a ball and I have a baseball bat—whack it way out to sea.

"Fear's in your mind, it's not a tangible thing. You therefore control it," he said.

This is a mind game I have so far won. I don't intend to lose now.

I trust *Sassy Jam*. She was built for this weather. I'm a sitting duck here though; my anchor isn't deep and *Sassy* could be dragged into shallow water. I decide to take charge and go on deck to sail her north. My father had taught me to navigate the old-fashioned way, using the sextant, the almanac, the stars, and the sun. I had to fight for my lessons as he hadn't believed a girl could solo sail or survive storms or were logical enough to work out the necessary calculations. Now I'm as good as Finn ever was. And tonight, with half my equipment damaged from the voyage to Samoa, I'm grateful for the hard-won lessons.

Before I can put on my safety harness, a blaring roar gallops toward us from the starboard side. I'm sure the hand of Neptune picks up *Sassy* and throws us down a wave. A locker door bursts open and its contents float in the bilge water. Yet another booming wave. I crash against the bulkhead. A starburst of pain cracks through my skull. I drop to the floor, settling in two inches of seawater. My head pulses, my clothes wet. *Here we go again.*

Objects zip around the cabin, working loose with the force of the knockdown. *Sassy* continues to roll. The mast must be in the water. It could break, a porthole might pop, the boat could crush in on itself. I had been here so many times already on this journey, this odyssey. The word 'journey' doesn't cut it. *Maybe I deserve to die. No need for police or courts or judges or my family's accusations. Maybe this is Neptune's justice.*

Sassy rights herself, groaning against the strain.

Urgently needing to check the mast, I head topside. Saltwater smashes into my face, sucking my breath away. The mast stands tall, a magic wand reaching into the sky. I whoop, then clip my harness on in three places. The ocean rages. Fat splatters of rain tip from the sky. Hunching low against the force of the waves that break across the cockpit, I cling to the helm. The accelerating rain stings every part of my exposed skin as if the clouds are hurling small, sharp rocks. A heavy layer of cloud cloaks the stars and moon. The darkness heightens the sound of the roaring waves and the sense that I'm inside a swirling black hole. This must resemble being in outer space, not knowing which way is up and which way is down.

I'd spent years imagining myself fighting one of the storms in the posters on my bedroom walls. When I'd sailed with my family, I always had to watch because I was too young and weak to have an important role during a storm. But I remembered everything.

"Check the horizon every twenty minutes," Dad had repeated.

"When sailing at night, lower your speed so you've got time to see hazards and take action," Uncle Brody said.

"Stand astride in big storms to keep your footing— pretend you're riding a horse . . . or your boyfriend," Finn said, though I hadn't had a boyfriend at that point.

"The ocean is both beautiful and deadly," Dad said.

"When you have a problem, pivot it around, stare at it from all directions so you find the right solution quickly," Uncle Brody said.

"The sea is the boss, except when I'm here. Then I'm the boss," Finn said.

Now I tick off my mental checklist, listen to the storm and to *Sassy*, then enjoy the rollercoaster ride. *My new world*. I'm not merely imagining being inside those sailing posters or watching my family from the safety of the bunk.

BY FOUR IN THE MORNING, the wind dies to fifteen knots, and I heave to. Staying under the protection of the dodger that covers the entranceway, mimicking a tiny outdoor room, the moisture-thick air wets my nostrils with every breath. The rolling mountain ranges of the Pacific Ocean are awe-inspiring. I leap onto the cabin roof and squint through spray so fine it could be powdered sugar. My world evolves until the sun appears to be a ball of fire floating in the silky waves.

The cabin has the air of a room recently struck by a hurricane. My nose stings from the seawater and salt burns the back of my throat and scratches behind my eyelids. I need sleep, in case the storm stirs up again, but I must tidy the cabin to protect myself from flying objects. I stow anything that has worked its way loose and come across the photo of my father as a boy, with his little sister who had died when she was young. The photo is black and white, the edges thin and frayed, as though someone has fingered it many times. Turning the snapshot over, I make out a scraggy cursive: David and Bridie 1978. It had been stowed on *Sassy* ever since I could remember. Frameless, it used to be wedged in a locker door. It had always seemed beyond belief that my father had ever been a sweet young boy. At some point, someone must have put the photo away because I hadn't seen it in a while.

When I'm so tired it's as if my body fills with cement, I unlatch the bunk and drop into it, hoping the storm doesn't circle back.

AFTER SLEEPING until midday to recover from the all-night squall, I work to sail through the shipping lanes at the top of Western Samoa, bruised and with heavy muscles. There are a lot of ships to avoid, and it's a slow sail, forcing me to stop in Uafato Bay for a second night on *Sassy*. At least the storm has retreated.

I wake the next morning to the sight of climbing hills of rainforest that rise and fall like turrets on a cliff-side castle. Ropes of salt-clogged hair rasp my cheeks so the first thing I do is take a cool shower in the head.

The run to Lalomanu Beach has a similar backdrop at Uafato Bay, and the fish resemble sparkling jewels above a honeycomb of coral reefs. *Sassy Jam* cuts through the waves, and I search for sea eagles. I love to watch them circle as if they're keeping me company and guiding me. The sense of happiness that bursts through me as I sail makes me believe

I've found the secret reason for living. *Being on Sassy is the only time I feel safe or like I belong on this earth. Or I can be myself.* I've always preferred invisibility, hiding in the school library or in study rooms at college. I should've been a mermaid. As Uncle Brody once said, flying below the radar is my thing. Yet the idea of seeing Drew again . . . My thoughts surge and climb and pick up speed, a wayward hot air balloon.

———

The Coconut Palm Beach Resort is on the edge of a translucent bay and consists of one central open-sided building and smaller groups of round thatched huts on the beach. Behind them rises the sheer cliff face of the island, overgrown with tropical plants and trees.

It's late morning when I lay anchor at Drew's resort. Humming to myself, I raid my mother's bag of clothes—still packed for her aborted voyage—to find something different to wear. I change into an emerald green bikini and a gold sarong then brush my hair in front of the foil-like mirror in the head. It's the first time I've allowed myself to use the mirror since I left America, unable to face myself. My arms are more muscled and I'm darkly tanned. I'm thinner too, and my hair is more than stupidly long—too noticeable and easy for someone to recognize me. I should've cut it when I first arrived. I pull it into a ponytail, grab the galley scissors, and chop it until it reaches the middle of my back. Somehow, I can't bear to cut it any shorter—then there'd be no hair curtain to hide behind.

Will Drew be happy to see me? It's taken longer to reach him than I'd hoped—two and a half days.

But it doesn't matter if he's happy to see me.

I'm here to fix the windvane. *No more kisses.*

I untie the sarong and replace it with my usual denim

shorts and a black tank top, rehearsing what to say. 'Thanks for the note. I really need to get the boat fixed so where do I find this boat guy?' *Too direct. Too ungrateful.* 'Thanks so much for helping me. I need to leave soon so I totally appreciate it. Is George far from here?'

Who am I kidding? I want to be kissed again.

CHAPTER 8

When I catch sight of Drew, he's leaning casually against a white marble pillar, chatting to guests who are sipping coffee at a table in the bar. He's wearing a navy polo shirt and khaki shorts, a uniform judging from the yellow logo on the pockets. The shirt hangs loosely over his stomach, reminding me of the chiseled muscles beneath. The thought makes me catch my breath. Never had I felt my breath hitch with Connor, even in the early days when he was kinder. Had I ever loved Connor? I realize now that he had most likely been a haven, an escape from home—my heart had been too deeply buried because of how my father treated my mom. But Drew doesn't fill me with wariness or trepidation; instead, my soul flutters, a wayward leaf in the trade winds.

All the words I had rehearsed to say to Drew trickle from my brain.

Drew's gesticulating and laughing with the guests, and a ton of envy wades through me because they get to be with him. The small group cracks up as if hearing a punchline. Drew then walks behind the ornately carved bar where a couple of men sit a few stools apart. He crosses to the swarthy one in the red short-sleeved polo shirt and serves him another beer. I'm a statue in the doorway, admiring his toothpaste-commercial smile. Do I walk in and say hello or wait outside until he's finished work or—

Drew stares directly at me.

I half-wave. As recognition cuffs him, he releases a guarded smile. He says something to his guest and stiffly beckons me over.

He's not happy to see me. Red-shirt man turns out to be Brett. He jumps to his feet and crosses to me before I can take three steps.

"If it isn't Gotta Go Girl." Brett's bushy eyebrows bow like question marks, and he puts his palm on the middle of my back, guiding me to the bar. He lets his torso bump me. "Have a seat. A cocktail for the pretty lady, bar man, before she vanishes again. Something bright and gorgeous . . . just like her."

I perch on the timber stool and peer at Drew shyly.

"Hey," Drew says through a small smile. He continues to mix a drink as if I'm merely a customer he met once, not the girl he kissed good night. *What was I thinking?* It was barely a kiss. It was a peck. Something you'd give your grandma. But it had felt so tender and—

"How'd you find us?" Brett asks.

I un-crease my brow and regard Brett, who's begging for my attention like a puppy. My hair slides across my face. Brett reaches to push it aside, but I pull back, and his hand swerves to pick up his beer instead.

"This is most definitely a major coincidence or are you stalking me?" Brett continues. He looks at me as if he knows there's bad in me somewhere, and it's only a matter of time before he finds it.

Too hurt by Drew's non-reaction to think of a quick retort, I say, "I'm here about a boat. What about you?"

"Keeping my good friend entertained. He landed a cushy

job here."

I inspect the beige-flecked marble floors, the white pillars, the huge silver ceiling fans, and the plush leather sofas scattered around the edges of the room. When I steal a glance at Drew, he's focused on slicing limes.

"So, you're into boats," Brett asks.

"Yup. And do you live here, too?"

"Nope. But not far from here. I landed an awesome pad in Saleapaga Beach."

I recognize the name as being where George lives.

Drew places a creamy drink donned with cherries, pineapple, limes, and a pink cocktail umbrella in front of me. "Here you go, Emily." I flinch at the name. Drew seems to wrongly interpret my reaction and murmurs, "Don't worry, it's non-alcoholic."

"What's that you say?" Brett jumps in. "I'm *not* an alcoholic." He clearly finds it impossible to speak without shouting and hates being left out. Drew and I smirk. Brett gapes from Drew to me. "Whatever, dudes. I need to go wrestle an anaconda." He scrapes back his stool and meanders through the tables in the direction of the restrooms.

Drew busies himself clearing the bar of empty glasses. I search for a clue in his face. *Is he mad at me?*

"You remembered your shoes today," I say. This time he gives me that easy smile, the one that reaches his eyes. *Whoa.*

"I thought you weren't coming." He picks up a tea towel to dry a row of glasses.

Is that what's bothering him? "I had supplies to buy, and it was a difficult sail across the north of the island. There was an overnight tropical storm."

"I asked George about that. He said it was short-lived and if you'd already crossed the Pacific, you'd be fine."

"Thanks for the note. Who was the messenger?"

"Amosa. He's a local who works at the shelter. He lives near where you anchored." Drew's expression unwinds and softens as he catches my glance. But then he lowers his gaze, and a glint of something sorrowful twists across his features. He half-heartedly pokes a sharp pick into a mound of ice. *Something's up.*

"I . . . I'm lucky to have made it through the shipping lanes. There were about a hundred ships playing target practice with me. It took longer than I had expected," I explain.

"And you had a makeover." He stares pointedly at my hair. "No wonder you took three days to get here." He lines up neat rows of glasses and a pink tinge flushes his neck.

He's been counting the days.

We hear Brett's stomping footsteps. Drew glares at him.

"What did I miss?" Brett says so loudly that you'd think he wanted the whole room to answer.

"Three rounds of shots and naked dancing girls," Drew teases, though he's not smiling. I smirk into my drink, which tastes of creamy pineapples. "I'm on my break soon. Do you want to wait, and we can have lunch?"

"Sounds good to me, Vega old boy," Brett says in a fake posh English accent. He scarfs his beer.

"Ignore him," Drew says, irritated. "He should've been born in 1930s England. And he believes he's James Bond."

"I should try to reach George," I say.

Drew watches as my hand wrings my wrist, worrying back and forth.

"Run along and work, boy," Brett says, flicking his fingers at Drew. "Leave us alone to talk, and I'll convince my beloved to stay for lunch." Drew's expression zips shut. Clearly, he hasn't told Brett about our evening together. *Or that kiss.* Drew moves to serve a new guest.

"How is the woman you took to the hospital? And Sienna?" I ask Brett.

"No idea." Brett shunts his bar stool closer. "Tell me everything about yourself. Do you have a boyfriend?" His dark eyes may be a little too close together, his chin vaguely pointed, his face slightly too long, but he's a big guy, and there's an intriguing buzz around him—a dangerous one even. Like he's a fallen angel.

"I'm betrothed to my boat," I say.

A skinny, pasty man with white-blond hair wearing the same uniform as Drew drops newspapers on various tables before stepping behind the bar. I hope none of them are headlining my story. The man wears a manager badge and asks if we want to order anything. His voice is toneless, and the waves of disapproval rippling from him could start a tsunami.

"We're fine, good man," Brett says. "I'll let you know when I run dry."

I cringe at Brett's manner and wonder if non-hotel guests can use the bar. And now Drew has disappeared. I cast around the restaurant.

"Have you got a job, too?" I ask Brett to keep him talking about himself.

"Christ, no. I'm on an extended holiday. Not like these wimps." He indicates to the skinny, pale man. From Brett's drawl, he went to a very posh school. Shame they didn't teach him any manners.

"Idle hands and all that," I say.

"I am the original naughty little devil, so that suits me." He runs his fingers through his dark hair and leans in closer. I hold my drink between us to keep him at bay. His grin is laced with sleaze. "Christ, you look fabulous today."

"He's not here." Drew is magically beside me. I startle. "I mean George isn't," he adds. "But you can call him from the office." His expression is all business.

I slip to my feet.

"Don't be long, mate," Brett says. "Emily and I were just getting to know each other."

He's unbelievably presumptuous. And pushy. I want to tell him so but follow Drew out of the bar and into a reception area which is filled with waterfalls, tropical plants, and ceiling fans the size of flying saucers.

"I spoke to George a couple of days ago," Drew says. He glances back at the bar and Brett, edgy. "He knows you might call. And Sienna's in the office."

What have I done wrong? If Drew assumed I'd ignored his message and wasn't coming, I've explained why I was delayed.

My throat is suddenly fat with fright.

He's recognized me from a news story.

Drew holds the office door open and greets Sienna. She's wearing a baby-pink dress, and she twinkles at him.

"It's Emily," Sienna exclaims, though I have stopped some distance from them, shocked by the possibility that Drew knows I'm *not* Emily. I wonder if I should run.

"Nice haircut." Sienna stares at me, hands on hips, her lips pinned into a half-smile. I will myself to stop acting jumpy, but too many people can identify me now.

I step closer and strain to keep my voice steady. "Thanks for letting me use the phone."

"It sounds as if you're in a bind." Sienna throws a huge smile at Drew. "Happy to help."

A surge of jealousy hardens my mouth. Maybe there's my answer—maybe Sienna and Drew are together now, and Drew's feeling awkward. I scrutinize the piece of paper with George's details. *Why do I feel like flotsam when other people are around Drew?* Except for that one time—that kiss.

I notice the cut on the side of Sienna's forehead. "How's your head injury?"

Sienna brushes her fingertips over it. "All fixed up. Still feel stupid though."

I peek at Drew over my shoulder, seeking eye contact.

"I'll leave you to it," Drew says. He touches my arm. "Meet you back in the bar." This time, I catch that look in his eyes—the private one that says, *I remember that kiss, too.* I wilt.

What game is he playing?

WHEN I RETURN to the bar, I feed my irritation with Drew. I refuse to be the timid self I used to be around guys, not after all I've survived to get here. If he knows something, he should tell me.

"No answer," I tell both Drew and Brett. I pull my stool away from Brett and perch, wishing Brett would leave so I could ask Drew, straight up, what's bugging him.

"Did you meet another of Drew's groupies?" When I frown, Brett adds, "Sienna. Another member of the DAC— Drew's Admirer's Club."

"Stop it, Brett." Drew's glare isn't joking.

"What? Haven't you told Emily about Ava? And your string of admirers."

"Who's Ava?" I ask.

"Seriously, Brett. Shut it. Ignore him, Emily. He's trying to get a rise. Ava is an *ex*-girlfriend." He shoots a sharp look at Brett. "Shall we go for lunch? You can try George again when we get back."

"Perfect," Brett drawls. He jumps theatrically from his stool and cruises out the bar ahead of us.

Drew follows behind me, so close. I hold my breath to contain the zips of electricity inside me.

"Where's your boat?" Drew asks as we descend to the beach. I point to *Sassy*, rising and falling with the small rollers.

"Awesome. Where'd you find her?" Brett asks.

"In Apia," I lie. "For a bit of island hopping."

Drew squashes a questioning frown before bending to take off his shoes. He chucks them under the stairs.

"On your own?" Brett squints into the sun.

"Yes. No big deal. It's easy when you know how."

Drew's gaze is lost in the horizon, probably wondering why I'm lying.

When we walk up the beach, it's like having personal bodyguards on either side of me, yet one is wary and polite and the other assumes he owns me.

"Want to play tennis later, mate?" Brett asks.

Drew shakes his head. "Not today."

"Are you good players?" I ask.

"I'm an undiscovered talent," Brett says while Drew snorts and Brett kicks sand at him. "I'll have you know I was nearly a ball boy for the Australian Open."

"You must be very talented," I say sarcastically.

Drew's mouth twitches. "Stick to surfing, mate. Playing you is comparable to playing an emu—all long legs and flapping." Brett shoves Drew who thumps him back. They resemble a couple of playful lions but with an undercurrent of competitiveness, ready to spill over into a rougher fight.

At the Beach Shack, Brett sucks the energy out of the café, talking non-stop, telling jokes, making the staff run in circles, and generally acting as if he's the only person in the room. Drew allows him the spotlight and remains backstage during the verbal tangos Brett draws me into. All the while, I can't figure out what's going on in Drew's mind—he probably thinks I'm into Brett.

"You checked your emails lately, mate?" Brett asks Drew.

Drew's face cramps. He quickly stitches a half-smile into place. "Nah. Avoiding technology these days."

"Avoiding your dad, more like. He's emailing *me* now."

Drew's chest expands slowly. He lets the air slip gradually from between his lips. "What's he saying now?" His focus remains locked on the skyline.

"You're going to screw things up, mate. He wants you home before the end of the month or—" Brett leaves the sentence hanging. "Or don't bother coming back. He's really mad now."

A pang of disbelief staples itself to Drew's features.

"I know it sucks, mate, but email him, would you? At least try to talk him around."

On the way back to the resort, Brett flings a heavy arm around my shoulders. I push it away and keep things light by teasing him for being shameless, but that only serves as a challenge, and he keeps putting a hand on my arm, back, or neck.

"Crap. I'm already an hour late." Brett glances at what seems an expensive watch. "Going surfing." He bends to kiss me goodbye. I twist so that he grazes my cheek. "Take care of her for me, Vega," he calls out, bounding up the beach stairs three at a time.

"He's so presumptuous . . . and sleazy," I say, wanting Drew to know I'm not interested. We stand facing each other, but stare at our feet.

Drew kicks at the sand between us. "He's a bit messed up, for sure."

"Given you've been friends all your life, you don't seem to like him much."

Drew's gaze flits to mine and back to the sand again. "Ignore me. It's just jealousy talking."

"Jealousy?"

Drew deconstructs the guarded mask on his face until his laidback grin reappears. "He's not the best wingman." Drew snorts. "Whenever we meet a girl, he turns competitive and muscles in, as if he's first in line. Like he's irresistible or something. A friend of mine back home, Jamison, said I should be flattered, except sometimes, it seems as if Brett's trying to be a copy of me. I don't usually care. It's not worth the confrontation. He's not had an easy life, so if it makes him feel better fine. But this time—"

He lets his gaze rove across my face and I find it again— the intimacy we shared at the harbor wall. Heat ripples through my belly.

"With you," he says, then pauses, as if rummaging for the right words, "I do care."

He likes me. My response snags somewhere in the maze of my brain. Silence dangles between us.

Drew chuckles stiffly then glances at Brett's exit. "I haven't told him anything about our . . . us." He watches *Sassy.* "It'd only make him worse and turn you into some sort of prize to be won."

There's an us? I dig my toes into the sand and watch them disappear. "Is that why you're, well . . . you seem distant." I can't believe my cheeks aren't beetroot or that I haven't taken off down the beach to *Sassy* yet.

"Sorry. Just keeping you out of his firing line. Make sense?"

"How's he not had an easy life? It sounds as if he's loaded and went to some private school."

"Yeah. It's not that simple. All the money in the world doesn't buy happiness." Drew chuckles. "Jeez, when you turned up and he was here, I got so mad. I couldn't believe my bad luck. He hasn't stopped talking about you, by the way. I reckon you made quite an impression on him."

"What, that I eat like a caveman? Besides, I think any girl makes an impression on Brett."

Drew shrugs but keeps watching me. An emotion, raw and powerful, roars in his eyes.

A sharp pulse shoots through me. *What's wrong with me? I need to focus on getting out of Samoa.* I break the moment by stepping away slightly and turning to stare at *Sassy.* The sight of *Sassy Jam's* familiar name slanting across her hull in raspberry-colored letters is reassuring.

Drew clears his throat. "Named after your dad's sassy daughter, then. But jam?"

"At the start of every sailing trip from back when I was a toddler, Dad would say, 'Don't forget the jam. We can cope with anything at sea so long as we have jam.' My mom had forgotten toothbrushes and swimsuits before, but our family would rather brush our teeth with a finger and swim in underwear than forego Dad's breakfast pancakes. We'd sit in the cockpit surrounded by the creamy dawn light and inhale several helpings of them, covered in lashings of strawberry jam. *Don't forget the jam* became a running family joke. When he bought *Sassy*, Dad added the word Jam to her name." I know I'm rambling, but my thoughts are whirring, doubling back around the twin desires to be kissed again and the need to get the hell out of here.

"Sounds as if you had a happy childhood."

I suppress a snort. But yes, it had once been happy. Before my dad started drinking. All the love and the hate I feel for him weave together and pull tight around me. But the dad I once loved died a lot longer back than a few months ago.

"I better get to work." Drew steps in front of me. I'm chained in confusion and by the expression on his face, so is he. "I didn't mean to be distant, and sorry about Brett. Have I scared you off?"

I peer past his shoulder at *Sassy*. "You know I'm not staying in Samoa for long—"

"Hopefully long enough." His voice is warm, caramel smooth, and he curls a pinkie finger around mine. Waves of heat stroll through me. *He doesn't realize who he's holding pinkies with.*

"I should try George again," I say and unlatch our pinkies. *Mind on the job.*

We walk up to the resort in silence, until Drew breaks it. "It was weird watching you paddle into the darkness that night." His tone is intimate, his words like secret, soft fingers stroking my cheek.

When we reach the bar and his hand briefly squeezes mine, I have to stop myself from grabbing on tight.

And breathe.

CHAPTER 9

As soon as we step inside the bar, the pale-skinned blond man I met earlier strides past us. "About time, Drew," he barks. Appearing heckled, he stalks out, moving so stiffly it's as if he recently stepped out of a freezer.

"What's his story? He's not very friendly," I say.

"Anton? He's the bar manager. Not a big talker. Power crazy. Want another cocktail? Sienna will be back in ten."

"Could I have some water, too?"

Drew digs into the ice with a silver scoop. "So, we return to the small talk you hate."

"Is that coming from Mr. Fear of Confrontation?" He frowns and rattles the cocktail shaker. "Brett," I explain. "Most people would've thumped him for being such a bad wingman."

Drew shuffles from one foot to the other. When he lifts his chin again, his expression is uneasy. "Am I being lame?"

"No. It's a bit unusual but I don't know about these things."

"Brett's faced a lot in his life. His mother left him when he was a baby, and it all went downhill from there."

"You might need to call him on it. You don't need to actually exchange blows."

Drew keeps slicing limes and chunking pineapple. "I'd much rather avoid *that* conversation. Too much water under the bridge. It sounds clichéd, but we're like brothers. We've leaned on each other."

"I reckon you're happier confronting stray angry dogs than people."

"Reckon you're right. More water?"

He shakes a wet glass and flecks of water sprinkle me. Chuckling, I wipe my face.

Drew places a perfectly decorated cocktail in front of me. "So how come you told Brett you picked up *Sassy Jam* in Samoa for island hopping?"

"You know I hate small talk."

He smirks. "But you enjoy lying?"

I chuck my cocktail umbrella at his pecs like a dart. He catches it and threatens to do the same.

"That's your answer?"

I shrug. "Whenever I tell people about my sailing, it leads to loads of attention. I prefer to fly under the radar. An invisibility cloak would be a perfect birthday gift for me." *Too many questions. This is exactly why I can't get friendly with Drew.* "Anyway, I better try George again." I take a long sip of the cocktail and scoot out the bar.

The office is empty, but I don't feel right using the phone without asking. Not ready to tackle Drew again, I slump on a sofa in the reception area and watch pairs of parrots flit across the high ceilings.

A cloud hangs in my brain like a wad of cottonwool. I need to pick at it to pull it apart.

I'm drawn to Drew in a way that's far more than an easy growing friendship. And it's not simply a craving for human contact after weeks at sea because I don't feel the same about Brett.

My train of thought crashes. *There can't be anything between us.* I can't get involved with Drew with all I have to hide from him—and the future I must face. *Prison.* I've lived my dream by solo sailing the Pacific, and I always knew that at the end of it, I'd be arrested and would have to prove that Connor, a supposedly model citizen, wasn't quite so perfect. But at least I'd have time to explain everything to my family, even spend a couple of final weeks or months together without the presence of my father or Connor. If I went to prison for life, I'd at least have that.

I need to become an ice queen when Drew's around. It isn't fair otherwise. It's not about whether to trust him anymore. I do trust him. *But how can I lead him on, knowing where this ends?* Time to focus, to fix *Sassy*, to sail to Townsville in Queensland—that's important, not some holiday romance. Besides, I'm my mom's daughter . . . men weaken me. *Love can never be for me.* I had vowed it as I crossed the equator. I squeeze my eyes shut. It's as if a passing rain squall dumped on me and swept away the restless thrill of Drew.

With my decision finally made, I return to the bar determined not to weaken my resolve in his presence. I immediately tell Drew I have jobs to do on *Sassy*. He's smiling, but the light behind his grin dims. Instead of going to *Sassy* though, I wander up the beach and out of sight, captured in melancholy.

IT'S NOT until four o'clock that I finally reach George. He sounds passionate about boats, even suggesting he'll make parts if he can't buy them on the islands.

"All sorted?" Sienna asks when I hang up.

"Yes. George thinks he'll have my boat fixed in a week."

"And then you're off to Australia?"

I nod, realizing that Sienna is checking how the land lies between me and Drew. It's clear she's interested in him, and I just turned up and spoiled her plans.

"Why Australia?" Sienna asks.

I keep it short. "My family moved there."

"How'd they get in? I've been trying to emigrate to Sydney for a while now."

I wonder if Sienna means emigrate *to Drew*. I mumble, "My mom and her brother were born there."

There's a long silence before Sienna says, almost to herself, "You're very brave."

WHEN I WALK into the restaurant, Drew is signing out of his shift. He comes to the guest side of the bar and moves *oh so close*. I'm startled when his pinkie finger wraps around mine again.

"Want to go for a swim?" he asks. "I know a great swimming hole nearby. The sea life is amazing. We've got two hours before the light goes."

"I'd love to, but I've talked to George and I have to sail *Sassy* to his place. He says he'll need to work on her between doing his other job. Apparently, he's 'a teacher of the art of surfing' when he isn't mucking around on boats."

"That's great. He can help, then?"

"Yes. Thanks for putting us in touch. He even has a jetty and a boat he can use to tow *Sassy* in." My voice is pitchy with excitement.

"How long will it take to sail there?" Drew's grip moves from my pinkie finger to grasp my whole hand. *Breathe, breathe.*

I should pull away, but it seems mean or rude. "An hour, he reckons."

"Quick swim first?"

"I can't." I peer over his shoulder at Anton and a couple of other guests at the bar. Now isn't the time to say what I must. "I need to get *Sassy* fixed or I'll never reach Australia." I keep my voice low, between us.

Drew straightens, releases my hand, and rests his elbow on the countertop. The muscles in his arm flex. "Sure thing." He zips an empty look out to sea. "I'll walk you to the dinghy." His tone is flat behind a reflective smile.

When we reach the beach, he pauses to take off his shoes. I mooch on, searching for the right words so I don't hurt his feelings. After he catches up, I stop and turn to face him. I take a deliberate step back to keep a large space between us, then make circles in the sand with my pointed foot. I wish I could become a cardboard cut-out of myself and fold myself until I'm so small the wind could whisk me away.

He reaches for my hand. "Did I say something wrong?"

"No, no." I take my hand back. "It's just . . . I've been waiting all day to contact George. I need to get there." The silence solidifies between us. "And . . ." I can't push the words out.

"And?" he asks.

The words are spiky in my mouth. I spit them out, "I-I like you. But I'm leaving Samoa in a week."

Drew rubs the back of his neck. "Do you have a boyfriend in LA?" His gaze collects mine. I shake my head. "You're sailing to Australia—a country I actually *live* in. Not the North Pole. Can we see where this takes us?"

He has a point. *If I wasn't wanted for murder.*

He opens his mouth to say something but heaves a sigh instead, his confusion marooned on his face. "I don't know much about you, but what I do know is you're as attracted to me as I am to you." His expression morphs to boyish.

An embarrassed smile explodes onto my face. "And how exactly do you know that?"

"Because . . ." He clasps my elbows, moves near enough

his nose is inches away, and his warm breath tickles my open lips. "When I get close to you, you stop breathing."

I laugh and pull back. He's taken a blender to my emotions.

"Am I going too fast for you?" he asks. "I probably am. But I've never felt like this. It's as if every moment in my life led me to being in that café, that stray scaring the tourist . . ."

I turn from him, stare out at *Sassy*. There are no words.

His chuckle is intimate, encircling my heart. He moves so we stand facing the ocean, our arms touching, sending a tickle deep into the core of me. "You know, this isn't small talk," he says. "This is serious stuff. You need to speak to me."

The silence thickens between us.

The only thing I do know is I don't want to lie to him anymore, and I don't want to let him get close only to hurt him later.

"I guess your silence *is* an answer," he finally says. I hear his long sigh but daren't look at him. Maybe this is the moment he'll reveal what's behind the surface and turn into Connor because he can't have what he wants. I brace myself for his angry words. *It's for the best.*

"Can I at least come aboard *Sassy Jam* . . . as a curious friend?" he asks. "I'm intrigued to see how you're crossing the Pacific. Is that allowed? Friends?"

Surprised, I glance at him. He's smiling still, but it's pitiful. When I don't respond to his request, he cuts off the smile —hurt and confusion scuttle across his features.

"Last one on the boat's a rotten egg," I shout and run down the beach toward *Sassy*.

I stride into the waves and hear him splash into the water behind. He overtakes me within a couple of strokes and beats me to *Sassy*. There, he roosts on her gunwale, shirtless, looking victorious. He reaches down to pull me aboard. Our bodies brush, slippery and wet. Desire, heated and sharp, puddles in every cell of my body.

"Hate to mention this, but the dinghy's still on the beach," he says. We're face to face, puffing and dripping a river of water into the cockpit.

"Hate to mention this, but you're still wearing your resort shorts."

"It's not as if you gave me the option to change. I'll fetch the dinghy. And my shirt."

"You'll need to paddle with the locker doors," I yell just as he steps onto the gunwale and dives in.

I watch him pull through the water. *Mind on the job.*

When he sculls toward *Sassy*, hair slicked back from the swim, naked to his shorts, he flings me an unguarded smile, and it's like all the air got sucked out of Samoa.

"No oars?" He lobs the dinghy's rope to me.

"A tanker gobbled one and a storm confiscated the other."

I tie him on and throw him a towel once he's aboard, which he knots around his waist. Then I show him the cabin and where I sleep, cook, and navigate using an almanac and a sextant. The whole time, I'm buzzing inside.

He draws me to tell him about the storms I survived, how the mushrooming ocean built into tower blocks that surrounded me. "The sun blazed through the grayness, a strobe light in fog, and for days, living on a boat was the same as living inside a washing machine. During the gales, I'd hang onto the handholds in here." I point as I speak. "Sometimes it felt personal, as if Neptune turned bully and was aiming forks of lightning at me. They struck into the surf so it was like the ocean was on fire beneath us. It was Neptune who crushed my windvane as easily as if it were a toy in his palm."

"I can't imagine being down here and going through that. It would be comparable to living inside an egg that's being tossed around by the waves." He grabs a handhold and I can see him picture how to cling on as the boat tips over. "Unbelievable. You're braver than me."

68

"Says you after your bungee jumps and crazy heli-snow-boarding."

"Different league. Not even close." The awe in his expression deepens.

It unglues me.

We're inches apart in the cramped cabin, and I wonder if he'll kiss me again. A squall of desire dumps on me. Abruptly, I say, "Guess I better get going." I leap up the three companionway stairs and go to set the sails.

Drew harrumphs onto the bench seat in the cockpit, looking adorably windswept. He studies his feet. I want to make him feel better without leading him on. I wonder if there's any harm in him coming to George's house. I'll be busy sailing and then George will be there. George could be a total crazy ass and I'd be stuck there, alone with him. Besides, on the beach, Drew said "friends only."

"Do you want to come for the sail to George's? You can get a taxi afterward." I instantly long to stuff the words back in my mouth. But they were easier to speak than saying goodbye.

"Sure." Drew's pensive expression dissolves into a grin. "I'm no sailor, though."

"It's okay. Sit on the cabin roof and enjoy."

I work the winches, knowing Drew's tracking my every move. As soon as I can, I grab a black hoodie to cover up. Shorts, tank top, and bikinis have been my go-to outfits since I was five, but now, with Drew watching me, it's as if my skin's too tight for my bones. Yet at the same time, I feel strangely elated. And strong.

CHAPTER 10

Sassy skims out of the lagoon toward George's home. An offshore breeze promises perfect sailing, and I stand tall at the helm with the wind pressed against me. The rush of water under *Sassy Jam* is calming. In a comfortable silence, Drew and I watch the sky change from blue to a kaleidoscope of pinks that darken until it looks like a dragon just breathed across the horizon, streaking the sky in flames.

I remain at the helm and opt to throw Drew a can of soda rather than go to him, just in case. The distance between us means we can't talk easily, but occasionally, we catch each other's glance. Drew's contains a note of melancholy.

After finishing his Coke, he pinches and twists the can, squashing it into a disc. He hops down beside me and offers to take mine. I tell myself to breathe.

"You're amazing," he says. "One day I want to sketch you, right here at the helm, doing your stuff."

The thought that such a day can never be, that what we could have had can never happen, creates an ache inside my chest the size of Australia.

My words, as usual, cajole and scuffle in my brain, so that nothing comes out of my mouth. The look he cradles me with is both wistful and searing. I have the urge to reach out and steady myself against him. Instead, I clutch at the helm.

Drew stays close and watches the sails but keeps looking back at me. *Into* me. As if he's trying to dig under my skin and bury something there. I feel certain that if I wasn't in charge of a sailboat, he'd have kissed me again. When he disappears below deck with the cans, I lift my face to the sky and pray the wind will wash away the ache.

George lives in paradise. His thatched, eggshell-blue timber cottage rests alone on snow-white sand, surrounded by palm trees that grow sideways across the beach, resembling a holiday postcard. Drew waves at someone who's walking down the jetty.

We anchor in deeper water as the light is deteriorating. I insist it's better if Drew watches while I work the winches and tie down the sails.

When I'm done, Drew jumps into the cockpit. "Sailing is mind-blowing. It's like moving through an untouched, spanking new world." *He gets it.* His smile is full sized. "And this is where *you* belong."

He gets me.

His stare digs into mine again. "I can't believe how . . . surprising you are. What you're capable of. It's impressive. But *you* don't think it's anything special. I'm really struggling not to kiss you. Sorry."

My legs feel as weak as wet spaghetti. "We did say friends only."

"I know. But I just don't see the problem. I'm so sure we were meant to meet. We can see what happens and if it's something we both want, then we can make this work if—"

"I'm just another person you've crossed paths with. One

of a hundred. One of a thousand. We're ships passing in the night. I have responsibilities."

He steps closer, slides his hand under my jaw. It's warm, and I resist the urge to place my hand on it. "Don't leave Samoa yet," he whispers.

I tilt my chin down, unable to hold eye contact. But still he moves closer, his breath in my hair as he kisses the skin between my eyebrows. Then both eyelids. Kisses as light as butterfly wings, but hot like the gusts of hot air pockets at sea. Inside, I'm quivering, heat is flurrying through me, but I gently push him away. He grasps my hands, scaring me a little. Connor had relished in rendering me helpless by gripping my wrists so I couldn't struggle. I look up to understand, but Drew's face is rife with confusion and longing. Desire flick-flacks, a fish on a hook. It's a moment that feels elongated, like days in the doldrums. Time loops.

Rather than return his gaze, *breathe,* I move away in silence, swing myself over the gunwale, and drop into the dinghy to paddle to George's jetty. Drew jumps in and acts as if that looping, out-of-time moment had never happened. He plays the fool and almost capsizes us over and over. Our horseplay means he brushes my arms, skims my knee, grabs my elbow, catches my waist. I am properly laughing, uncorking bubbles of too-long-trapped happiness that rise inside me like fizzing soda, and I don't care that I enjoy the feeling of Drew's hands on my salt-powdered skin.

A MAN of about fifty sits on a striped deck chair, beer in one hand, pipe in another, and an ice-cooler at his feet. He chuckles at me and Drew's antics. Thick set, and with a mop of dark hair speckled with gray that looks as if it's been hacked with a knife rather than cut by a barber, his leathery skin is deeply tanned, making him appear more Australian than English. The pockets of his long khaki shorts are bulging—one has a wad of surfboard wax sticking out and another, two screwdrivers and a bunch of keys. His chocolate-brown T-shirt shows a sketch of London Bridge.

"Welcome, welcome. Jus' in time for sundowners." His twang makes him resemble a character out of an Oliver Twist movie.

Drew scrambles onto the jetty, stoops, and clasps my wrists to help me up. I shake George's hand, and he passes us both a beer.

"Come, come," he says and, ignoring his deck chair, plunks himself on the end of the jetty. Drew and I follow and sit next to each other, our bare feet swinging above the breaking waves. I sip from the bottle once and grimace. When I put it aside, I catch Drew watching me, a lopsided grin strolling across his face. It's a moment of intimacy that flip-flops my heart.

Drew talks to George about London. It turns out he spent time there a few years ago. They make easy jokes about the climate and cucumber sandwiches, and I'm happy to quietly listen in on their conversation. Drew also mentions that Brett lives nearby, and that he plans to visit him later.

"You can phone a taxi from my place," George offers. He passes out another round of beers, though I politely refuse.

When Drew moves the topic to *Sassy* and Australia, George asks for stories of my voyage. I tell them about the time I woke to find myself staring into the iron wall of a gigantic tanker. I'd fallen asleep without switching on the running lights, so the tanker hadn't spotted *Sassy Jam*. It was also the last time I ever forgot to set the AIS alarm, which I explain to Drew, warns of other vessels in the area.

"It's about as loud as an air raid siren," George says.

"How come the tanker didn't see you on their radar?" Drew asks.

"Small boats don't show. We resemble flotsam on their

radar. And ships can't exactly jam on their breaks and stop if the captain sights you at the last moment."

Drew looks at me like I'm from another planet. "What did you do?"

"The engine was out, and unfurling the sails was pointless because the tell-tale ribbon on the mast promised there still wasn't any wind. That's how I lost my final paddle—the surf created by the tanker snatched it out of my fist. But then I realized the distance between *Sassy* and it was growing because the tanker's wake was shoving us aside. Then it glided away, a floating skyscraper."

"Jeez. I'm so impressed right now," Drew says. "How did you ever sleep again?"

"I didn't that night. I was too wired. And it was so hot. I sat in the cockpit under a sliver of moon for company, and I thanked the universe. The heavens were so full of stars it was like a child had been playing with glitter glue." I marvel at what a chatterbox I've become. Or a storyteller.

The ocean has changed me. Or maybe Drew has.

George sucks on his teeth. "Not sure I'd let my daughter start a solo campaign to Australia this time o' year though."

"I've managed the worst of it," I say. "This is the short leg, and there are loads of islands around if I need help."

"Bu' we'll be into cyclone season before you know. Don't get yourself caugh' up here too long, eh?" He inspects Drew, then chugs his beer.

Drew's face is stiff with alarm. "When's cyclone season start?"

"I've got at least a month's grace, surely," I interrupt.

"Maybe, bu' anytime from now onward. The usual weather windows have shortened 'cos the weather patterns have gone mad lately. El Nino . . ."

In silence, we take in the view where a million stars scatter themselves around a fat moon.

"Better get *Sassy* all fixed up fast then," I say.

George has given me a reason to quit Samoa as soon as possible, eliminating Drew's hope of me staying. I won't risk being caught here, in a country whose legal system could be dubious. I picture lazy dinners filled with great food and laughter with my family in Australia, walks on the beach, getting to know my brother again. Finn and I had once been close. We could sail together without the barking negativity of our father spoiling the joy of it. We could make memories that may sustain me when I'm locked up for life.

I turn to reiterate George's words to Drew, to make him understand the urgency of my departure, but Drew's face is crammed with everything but understanding.

He plunks his unfinished beer on the jetty and sizes up *Sassy*. "Maybe you should stay here until after the cyclone season. March, isn't it?" I fake laugh. Drew doesn't join in. "What's the point of risking your life when you've come so far?" His stare pins me to the spot.

That's six months away. "I can't. I'll be fine. *Sassy* and I have surfed fifty-foot waves."

"What can happen to a boat in a cyclone, George?"

"Phew." George sounds as if he's about to predict the end of the world. "Not worth thinkin' about."

"I've seen what a cyclone can do on land," Drew continues. "The village I mentioned, the one I'm helping rebuild. Homes were transformed into matchsticks, cars flung onto roofs, people tossed like puppets to their death. Imagine what damage it could do at sea." He fastens his gaze on me again, but this time I send an angrily charged stare back.

The night air between us turns brittle with hostility.

Who does he think he is? He's behaving in the same way my father did with my mother, trying to control me. Like Connor, who'd even limited my sailing time. I'd received many bruises from riling against that. So many it meant I had to give up mountain biking to find time for sailing. But it was worth fighting for. *I won't let Drew stop me from leaving Samoa.*

A chunky silence bulges between us.

George bites down on his pipe. "Right. Better call it a night." He struggles to his feet. "Ah, muscles gettin' old. You're welcome to a bed indoors, Emily, love. I've got a spare room."

Drew and I stand, awkward.

"Thank you, George. But I'm fine on *Sassy*," I say.

"Right then." George folds his chair. "I'll be round first thing to tow *Sassy Jam* in an' Doctor George can examine her." George chortles and lobs his empty beer bottles into the ice- cooler. "Come in when you're ready to make that phone call, Master Drew."

Drew scrapes his grim gaze from my face. "Thanks, George. I'll bring the ice box in a minute." He folds his arms.

The tension reaches a popping point while we wait for George to amble up the jetty, Drew's oppressive glare planted on me.

I take in a deep breath. "Thanks again for helping me find George." I keep my voice even, desperate for him not to become angry. I step backward, putting more distance between us. "Are you going to see Brett now?"

Drew's gaze is intimate and ringed with concern. "Why would you want to take the risk? What's in Australia that's so important?"

"George is exaggerating. I'll be fine. Anyhow, I must set up *Sassy* for the night now."

The moon casts enough light to reveal Drew's wounded expression through the shadows.

"What's the rush?" he asks. "Why do you need to leave so soon?"

Antagonism spikes my blood, my limbs become rigid. "Because I want to, Drew. That was my plan—to cross the

Pacific. And I don't need some guy I've spent a few hours with telling me what to do."

"Some guy? Gee, thanks." His jaw, firmly set, flexes from side to side.

"I'm not one of your groupies." The words are torn from my throat before I can close my mouth.

"Groupies? Jeez, you shouldn't listen to anything Brett says. You know he's competing for you."

The air snaps and crackles as if there's a feral animal between us.

"I really don't care how many girls there've been. My priority is to reach Australia."

"Well, this *insignificant* guy doesn't want you to do something stupid and—"

"Do you realize you sound like your father—telling me what to do, trying to control my life?" The words sprawl into the space between us, building a barrier.

His arms drop to his sides as fast as his jaw. "That's about the worst thing you could ever accuse me of. I am nothing like him—"

"Then stop bullying me and leave me to make my own decisions." I take three quick strides across the jetty and leap down into the dinghy.

As I wrestle with the tether, Drew's face hovers above me. "Emily, don't."

"Just leave me alone. Australia is my number one priority. I don't want a holiday romance. So, thank you for your help, but I think it's the end of the road." I push off without looking up.

It's the right thing to do. *Less lies, less hurt.*

When the dinghy bumps into *Sassy*, I dare to peek over my shoulder. The silhouette of Drew marches away.

And my heart follows him up the jetty.

CHAPTER 11

Two days later, *Sassy* is moored to George's jetty and repairs are progressing, but so slowly it's like watching coral grow. Worse, the engine has water damage. George is waiting for ordered parts and is searching for others. He says he's working as fast as he can to get me going before the weather worsens. Despite his good intentions, being around George puts me on edge because in contrast to Drew or Sienna, George has access to a TV screen—there's a satellite dish the size of a planet on the front of his cottage. At least none of them know my real name.

I'm miserable after the argument with Drew, but I handle it by keeping busy. Over the years, I have learned to use distraction to stop myself from thinking thoughts I didn't want to have, to block out feelings.

"Suck it up," I tell myself while tightening the alternator belt. I'd just scrubbed out the bilge and taped chafe points. Yesterday, I had crawled through every space below deck, checking for cracks and leaks. I de-rusted the winch, screws, and safety rails, and even the zipper on my denim shorts. Blisters and small cuts cover my hands, but I don't care. *I'm* doing the maintenance, not Dad or Finn. I'd watched them often enough, but my dad had always instructed me to wipe down the galley, tidy lockers, or wash dishes while they did the repairs.

But keeping busy doesn't have its usual effect. Every time I think of Drew—about every third minute—I'm crushed all over again. Not because I made it clear I didn't want a holiday romance, but because our final exchange was full of antagonism. *And I miss him.* I miss how he listened to me as if he cared. I miss how I felt comfortable talking to him. How he made me feel strong when I told stories of my voyage. How he treated me with such tenderness.

An achy, stretchy pressure pushes deep into my bones, and there's a strong sense of something lost. Like I'm incomplete. Although the pull to be near Drew is unfathomable and irrational, I can't stop it. Being weak and being manipulated like Play-Doh is in my genes.

I go for beach runs as if it's a punishment until my lungs burn, and I'm sucking in air so hard I nearly swallow my tongue. I search for sea glass for the wind chime George is making, except I search so avidly for the blue and green glass, smoothed by the tides, it's as if they're ancient lost treasures instead of broken bottles or lost items from a shipwreck. But the hollow of loneliness is still there, the pull of Drew still potent.

George offered the use of his facilities, accepting my desire to sleep on *Sassy*, but refusing to believe any woman wouldn't want a real bath or shower. I languish in the bathroom while George is at the surf school, a luxury no one understands until they haven't seen hot water running from a tap in over two months. George's cottage is as cluttered with bric-a-brac as a second-hand shop, yet the only picture decorating the room is a portrait of a young woman. It's a striking painting, covering half the wall. She's fair-haired and wears a baggy green blouse and white shorts, her legs dangling from a jetty above a pebble beach. She's staring out to sea, which is a darker gray than the clouds above. Conceivably, she was his wife.

His cottage is always unlocked, but today, the door has been left partly open. The sight transports me back to that last day at Stratton Hall. I had known the fact the door was ajar was ominous, yet I still went inside. I recall thinking that at least I didn't have that heart-pounding, wincing moment when I heard Connor's key in the lock, which in hindsight, was an odd thought—he was already inside. I had pushed the door open, and it banged into the tray of food I had prepared for Connor the night before. He had been unwell, so I made him chicken noodle soup, suggesting he ate it in bed. I decorated the tray with a folded napkin, his best cutlery, and a red tulip from the apology bouquet he had bought me. He hadn't touched the food, and the flower wilted in the bowl of soup and floated pathetically like a burst party balloon.

The next morning, Connor rushed to work early, prompting me to sneak out for a half-day of sailing. Connor wouldn't let me have a job, and he expected me to 'play house' all day. But he came home after lunch, and in leaving the tray on the floor in the hall, he was indicating his displeasure that it hadn't been cleaned up. After I closed the door, shutting out the last scowling light of the day, I listened for signs of Connor's mood. Was he working, sleeping, or getting drunk? But the storm that had been brewing all morning arrived, and rain flogged the windows and cocooned the house, making it hard to hear anything but the weather. Out the window, the wind had the bushes in its grip. They lunged from side to side, occasionally battering the windowpane.

TODAY, the hollow inside me is worse than yesterday. I set about tidying and come across the bags of my parents' clothes at the back of the aft storage—one oversized bag for each of them for their canceled voyage. I bite on my rolled lips and rub the heel of my hand across my sternum. I feel like crying—for my mother, my father, Connor, myself . . . I'm not sure. Maybe for everything that is now gone. What's left of my fighting spirit drains away. Too languid to carry on tidying, I poke around for more books and find my favorite atlas. My love of maps reignited, I settle in the cockpit with a bar of chocolate and pore over familiar pages, getting lost in dreams of foreign countries.

From the middle of the book, several pieces of paper slip out.

I recognize my dad's handwriting. I unfold the first sheet, my breath clipped inside me.

Dear Finn.

My father and Finn hadn't spoken in seven years. My hand trembles so at first, I can't make out the words on the shaking paper.

I know you hate me. As I hated my father for the same reason.
Your eyes are full of disappointment. You make me hate myself more. I deserve it. I was wrong about college, too. But I wanted you to be the best you can be. I didn't want you to give up and limit your choices. College saved me for a while. It gave me options. Maybe you don't need saving so it's okay you've gone to build boats. Possibly you'll be happier for that simpler life. I'm grateful Brody is there for you. He'll be a better father than I was. I'm sorry we fought. I wish I had your strength. I wish you luck.
Love you, son,
Dad

I take in a shivery breath and flatten the note against the

pages of the atlas. My father sounds so unlike himself. Depressed even. As if he's given up.

The next letter is addressed to me. My pulse stampedes as if my father's about to jump off the page and grab me.

My Dear Shae,
I don't know what to say. The bitterness in your face when I
see you . . . You are my mirror. In you I see how badly I
failed. It makes me weep. There are no words. Except I'm
sorry.

There's no sign off. Possibly he hadn't finished it. Were these the letters he intended to leave behind before he left on *Sassy?* I finger a third sheet, then unfold it like it's made of delicate firefly wings. It's addressed to my mother.

Darling Kathleen,
I know you stood by me, despite knowing how broken I was.
Despite my secrets. There aren't many women as incredible
as you. And I was the lucky sod who got to find you. You
never pushed me to reveal them. But it's time.
When my father became violent, gripped by the scruff of the
neck by alcohol, he broke me and sucked out all that was
right in me. I presumed I could escape. I believed I could
create a different future for myself. I should have known I
couldn't escape because there was too much hate and anger
for him, for myself. For my mom. Because she didn't stop
him from hitting her, either. Yet maybe you and she were
similar—you wanted to heal your beloved with your love.
The monster that lived inside my dad buried itself deep
inside me. I tried to fight it. Please believe I did. For you.
For years. But it lived in me, took over, ate away all that
was left of the good inside me until I was a replica of him.
If it helps, know that every time I struck you, I hated myself
more.

*I've never told anyone this, but Bridie jumped out of a
second-floor window. She was running from our father. I
killed her because I told her to run. I screamed at her to run
and never stop. Even the open window didn't stop her from
running. She was that afraid of him, and I didn't protect
her. I have taken on the responsibility for her death since
that day.*

Bridie. Dad's sister. He always refused to talk about her.
We only knew that she died young. A flame of sympathy
ignites for my father—or perhaps it's a flame of understanding. But then another thought makes me feel sick. My father
had done to my mother exactly what his father had done to
his mom. People can't help but grow up to be like their
parents. It's in our DNA. I always dreaded being like my
mom and then I became her when I was with Connor. I had
also hidden the bruises with makeup and pretended our relationship was happy. Tears prick, and I vow, again, to never
fall in love. History cannot repeat itself.

I try to keep reading the letter but must wait for the tears
to clear so I can see the handwriting.

*Sorry isn't a big enough word, my darling. Remorse, regret,
guilt are all that are left inside me, which means I have
nothing left to give. So, I must leave. I leave out of love—to
give you hope and a future that's full of happiness.*
*At least this way I can't hurt you anymore, and I'll enjoy
one more sea voyage before I can be with my sister again.
I didn't forget the jam.*
*Move forward. Know you were the highlight of my life.
Hate me if it helps but try to remember some of the good
times.*
All my love forever,
David

I hunch over the atlas, hug the letters to me and sob—it's worse than sobbing, gushing—but it releases a pressure valve. After a while, I search through the lockers for the black and white photo of my father and Bridie. This time I truly study it. The dark-haired boy of about nine, his hair swept in a severe side-part as if someone painted it on, is looking down fondly at a little girl, possibly half his age, like she's his favorite kitten. Her hair is a scruff of blond curls, and she stares into the camera, her face bland, but her eyes alert, knowing. I picture my father as a small boy, more afraid of his father than I had been, watching his sister jump to her death. It doesn't excuse what my father did to his family, but it explains it. And the side of me that isn't crazy angry with him—the side that loved sailing with him, that loved his passion for the sea, his confidence against the elements—understands a little more, and I no longer despise myself for both loving and hating him.

LATER, when I calm down, I lie in the bunk and read the letters again. *And I can be with my sister again.* He had planned to deliberately set off on *Sassy* without my mother. And it sounded as if he was never going to return. I wonder how he planned to join his sister. By drowning at sea? Or using the gun that's wrapped in an emerald-green towel and stored in the locker above the nav station.

It's ironic—his plan meant when I ran away on *Sassy Jam*, the boat was stocked with food, water, tools, and supplies, even toothbrushes and a Ziploc bag containing $10,000 in cash to add to the $500 I had taken from Connor's wallet. And everything was in working order. Apart from the fact there was no fuel onboard. Without a motor, I was forced to sail the entire trip, making it harder to circumnavigate storms and ensuring *Sassy* got stuck in the doldrums for weeks. But my father's suicide mission had aided my escape.

The sense of release from the past is liberating—I've had a scarf too tightly wound around my throat, in fact my entire body, and after reading the letters, it has loosened and drifted away in the breeze. I feel like that scarf—weightless and soft.

Reading these letters might help my mother. It could help her understand her husband a little better. Knowing he was sorry must surely help. I wonder if Connor was ever sorry.

The letters show that none of Dad's behavior had been our fault—we had not somehow enticed his rage. The letters could help Finn comprehend our father, if not forgive him. Maybe he could hang on to the good memories, not just the bad ones. Or he could let go of any regrets. These letters could help them all heal a little. *Sassy* and I *must* reach Queensland safely, or the truth will die with us.

"I'll deliver your letters, Dad." It will make up for wishing my father was dead and for being relieved when he was.

I stare through a porthole as if scanning for his specter in heaven. A feathery afternoon light casts shadows in the cabin. Tears dry, salty and stiff on my cheeks. Folding the letters along the exact same creases, I tuck them into the atlas, then slump on the bunk. I hug myself, craving a cuddle from my mother or a smile and joke from Finn. I think of Drew, let myself remember that look he gives me, the one that makes me feel as if I'm being bathed in sunlight. No one has ever looked at me that way—as if he deeply cares. Like I'm special.

Bogged in self-pity, I force myself to fix a broken locker catch.

"Ahoy there." *Sassy* rocks when someone jumps aboard. "Fit guy coming through." I jerk and bump my head on the locker door. It's not George's voice . . . or Drew's. *How dare he come aboard!*

85

I'm still rubbing my sore head when Brett pokes his shoulders through the hatch. "Did I make you bang your noggin?" He belly laughs and plunges into the cabin to rub it for me.

I step away and perch at the nav table, working to control the surprise on my face and brushing at the tear tracks on my cheeks.

"How's it going, Gotta Go Girl?" He looks dressed up in black jeans and a white, long-sleeved, linen shirt, one button too many undone.

"Good. How are you . . . both?" After what Drew said, Mr. Presumptuous needs reminding that I'm not his property. Although, after the last couple of days, especially the last couple of hours, a part of me is glad to see him.

"Drew said you were set up here with George."

At the mention of Drew, I want to ask how he is, but don't.

"So boring though," Brett adds. "No bars, no restaurants, only beach and more beach. I'm heading to Savaii soon. I need some noise. All this quiet is hurting my head." He leans against my bunk, jigging his left leg as if keeping time to a manic music track. "What's George fixing?"

I explain a few things, but his features glaze over. So, I change the subject. "What have you been up to besides making me bang my head?"

"Remember my mango head? I owed you." He winks and bends to peer through a porthole. He's huge in the small space, resembling a giant standing inside a treehouse. "What have I been doing? Surfing, drinking, siestas . . . What else is there to do round here?" His greedy inspection trails down my bikini-clad body.

I reach for a towel. "What about Drew? Will he move to Savaii with you?"

"Yeah. He's only filling in for someone at the resort. Another three weeks. He wants a job on the tourist boats that visit the reefs. More up his alley. But those jobs are hard to get." Somehow, I'm hurt that Drew didn't tell me this. "I'm going to have a bite to eat with some friends. Thought you'd want to come. I've got my car. It'll be fun." He resembles a nodding clown as he beams, willing me to say yes.

I hide behind my shield of hair. Alarm bells ring. Every part of me jumps to go, to escape the loneliness, to stop wallowing. *A distraction.* I squash the doubts; it'll be fine with others around—some friends out to dinner. There's invisibility in that. Except what if Drew's there? After Drew's warning about keeping me out of Brett's jealousy-fed firing line, I can't ask the question. But Brett would've mentioned if Drew was coming. I scrutinize Brett's expression of forced innocence and remember what Drew said about him having a tough time in the past. I imagine Brett's bravado is nothing but a screen for some deeper hurt, and I appreciate the need to hide behind screens.

"On one condition." I wind a strand of hair tightly around a finger.

"And what could that possibly be? That I don't leave your side all night?" He wiggles his bushy eyebrows ridiculously fast.

"This is not a date. Got it? Just friends. One wrong move, and you're toast."

"Done. You're too ugly for me anyway."

I laugh, even though I'm half-shocked. "I need to change first."

"I'll turn away, honest." He smirks, his dark brows pushed high.

"*Out.*" I shoo him up the steps. "I'll meet you at George's cottage."

BRETT IS A LUNATIC DRIVER. He steers with one hand on the

wheel, and I hang on grimly, sometimes banging into him as we round corners. The tires squeal, and a protective arm shoots across my breasts. *Is this his game?* With little to choose from, I had to make do with wearing my smartest white shorts and a black halter T-shirt with a black halter bikini top as a bra. Now I wish I'd worn a tracksuit.

He glances at me mid-screech, teeth flashing like a smiling shark. "I hope you enjoy dancing with the devil." His eyes sparkle with sin.

After twenty minutes, we swerve down a road that passes the Coconut Palm Beach Resort. I hadn't realized we were having dinner so close to where Drew works. My pulse jumps. Brett zips into a sandy parking lot, sliding into a space like a stunt man.

"There'll be four of us," he says as we climb out of the car. "I found a date for Drew."

My breaths resemble staples attaching to my chest. "You didn't say Drew was coming."

"You didn't ask."

I bite back a retaliation.

Drew isn't exactly pining for me then. I search for a taxi, but the parking lot is deserted.

CHAPTER 12

Brett links his arm with me and practically drags me across the parking lot. *Will Drew even talk to me?* Possibly we'll find a way to part on friendlier terms.

The restaurant is next to Drew's resort, only higher and nestled in a rainforest that rims the beach below. It's casual and open-aired with bubbling water features. Dark-green vines splashed with thousands of fairy lights weave between the roof beams. Muted TV screens broadcast a rugby game. If I'm headlining on the news, this dinner will be a disaster.

Brett saunters across a glossy bamboo floor with me in tow. I smile wistfully at the pianist behind the gold baby-grand piano, his shoulders pumping out the jazzy music he's playing. The restaurant reminds me of one we visited as a family in California, except the bar itself is modern—all mirrors and lights, a glowing lighthouse in the center of the room. Brett steers me toward it, his hand resting on my butt.

"*Brett,*" I say between gritted teeth, pushing him away, "*just friends.*"

"And I'm just being *friendly,*" he says. I glare at him, but it only makes him chuckle. "Besides, I'm the son of a lawyer. You should've got it in writing before you stepped into my car. What you wanna drink, Gotta Go Girl?" He's full of dangerous mischief. It's like being locked in a cage with an unpredictable lion cub.

Despite asking for ice water, Brett passes me a glass of champagne with a flourish. Ignoring my protests, he links arms and guides me through a room sprawling with dinner tables and comfy sofas. People look up as we pass and I hide behind my hair.

When I spot Drew, I do a double-take. He's sitting at a table with his arm around Sienna, his head bent close to hers. I can't unglue my stare. *Two days?* He moved on quickly. What happened to "we were meant to meet?" I fasten my popped-open mouth but can do nothing about the surge of both sadness and fury that quivers through me. I've been pining after a guy who's already moved on. *I'm such an idiot.*

As Brett yanks me forward, my feet taking tiny steps, Drew bends closer to Sienna, cuddling her small frame and stroking her back. I instantly know what the phrase, "to get one's heart ripped out," means.

I blew it. Drew's moved on. Why shouldn't he? I told him I wasn't interested. And that's the moment Drew looks up and notices me.

His expression screams discomfort. He straightens, frowning and failing to hide his displeasure. I should leave. I'll phone for a taxi. But I don't know George's address, and I doubt Brett will play ball.

Brett's eyes narrow. "Come on, Gotta Go Girl, smile. You're with me, remember?" Brett leads me forward, patting the hand he has clasped tightly in the crook of his elbow.

Drew's expression is intense, boring into me, then Brett. As Brett and I pause to negotiate our way around a table of people, I'm aware of the pull between me and Drew—an invisible Jesus line drawing taut between us. When Drew stands, the line tightens. I forcefully retrieve my arm from Brett, step behind him, sip air.

Brett surges forward to slap Drew on the back. "Vega, mate. Sorry we're late. Had to pick up Emily. What's with Sienna?"

I push my focus to Sienna whose face is pink and puffy.

"She's had some bad news." Drew's deadpan expression meets mine. "Remember the white dog at the shelter, when Sienna fainted?" Sienna lets out another sob, and Drew sits to put an arm around her shoulders again. "It was a hit and run. The dog didn't make it."

Sienna leans on her elbows, her face in her hands.

"Got pretty attached, didn't you?" Drew says, rubbing her back. He seems to be gently scolding her. "Sienna's been visiting the shelter a lot over the last few days."

Brett pulls out a chair for me and sends an impatient glance in my direction. My anger flares—he manipulated me into being his date. I shoot him a disapproving glare in return, but he's too busy clicking his fingers to catch the attention of a passing waiter.

"I'm so sorry, Sienna." My voice wobbles as I sit down.

"Best cure for misery is champagne," Brett says.

"She was so similar to the dog I had as a child," Sienna says, somehow able to stay cute even when she's crying—she looks like a heartbroken fairy. Her mint-green, gauzy dress adds to the effect. "I named this one Duchess, too." She sniffs.

Drew rubs her crouched back and dispatches a napkin. "Have some water."

She takes the glass he pours her and hiccups into it.

"Sorry. No one else understands." She half-smiles at Drew.

This is what you asked for. This is how it should be. Men and relationships are not for you. I repeat the words until I believe them, until some of my anger seeps away. But disappointment toes at my heart like a lost schoolboy.

Brett pours champagne for everyone. "Wash the tears away with this."

Tonight, I don't care that I stopped drinking a few years ago. The champagne prickles my tongue, then skids and burns inside my stomach. I gulp down more, but choke on the bubbles, which infuriates me because it makes Drew stare.

We're seated boy-girl, so I have Brett on one side and Drew on the other. Drew's dressed in a black casual shirt, opened at the collar, and Army-green jeans. I keep my gaze down while Brett attempts to cheer up Sienna with rude schoolboy jokes. Drew has flicked off his canvas slip-on shoes under the table. One bare foot rests on top of the other. He leans back in his chair, opening his stance. His knee touches mine. When I glance up, his blue eyes pierce into me, so intense they seem to push me into my seat. I collect myself, arms and legs pressed together, as if zipping myself into a straitjacket.

What's with the eye grilling? He's with Sienna now. Although I wouldn't put it past Brett to have set Drew up, too. The thought tugs. It could be true. And Drew was simply comforting Sienna. What else was he meant to do when she was so upset? I peek at him. He's swirling his champagne, staring reflectively into it. Then he looks up and catches my gaze before I can hide it.

"How are you?" His voice is low.

My heart jumps like a frog in a box, and I guzzle champagne. "I'm fine, thank you. How's the stray we brought in?"

"She's going to be all right."

I let my hair fall across my face and peer at Sienna. I can't bear Drew giving Sienna the attention I once received. I consider stabbing myself with a fork as an excuse to get out of there.

Brett dominates the spotlight, clearly his favorite place to be. He's a presumptuous lady killer, attentive to the needs of both me and Sienna, as if hedging his bets. Repeatedly, he places a hand on some part of me—a thigh, arm, elbow, or shoulder. And he's obnoxious when he orders my food without asking. I appreciate what Drew said though—it's not worth the confrontation. Somehow, it's all a sad performance, something harmless Brett hides behind. Except I feel like a prize ostrich when I find myself staring into the *giant* fillet steak Brett ordered for me.

"Thought I'd teach you how to cut meat with a knife and fork. Sienna, when we met Emily, she was tearing into a hunk of pork with her teeth, sauce dripping down her chin—"

"It shows she has a certain hunger for life," Drew interrupts. I quietly turn cherry red. "Emily has a lot of stories from her sailing," he adds. "Can you tell us one?"

"I've told you all the good ones," I say, clipped. I'm not in the mood for talking.

"You must have a shark story?" Brett urges.

"Sure," I say. I recall the fear I fought as the torpedo-shaped shark targeted *Sassy*, so close I could see its quivering gill slits and the white of a bullying eye. There was a creamy scar on its snout. I had no idea if it could ram *Sassy* or take a bite out of her. "One seemed to be gunning for me. Kept circling us. I had to shoot into the water to scare it away." The gun had smacked my palm and I stumbled backward, ears ringing. An acrid smell swamped my nostrils.

"You have a gun on board?" Drew asks.

"Of course."

"How big was the shark?" Sienna asks.

"At least ten feet long." I move pieces of steak around my plate, my appetite shot.

I'm grateful Brett turns everyone's attention back to him, and he becomes a swashbuckling storyteller. His anecdotes command center stage and distract from the fact that I've barely touched my food.

"Waiter, waiter, my good man. Please. More champagne. We're parched over here." Brett's grin is so infectious even the waiter doesn't seem to mind his clicking fingers. But it's impossible to keep track of how much I've drank. I ask Brett for water, and he refills my glass with more bubbles while launching into another story. When Drew excuses himself, interrupting Brett, I can't help but watch him, his broad frame surefooted as he walks across the room. A couple of girls turn their heads to track him, as does Sienna. He stops at the bar before going to the toilet and moments later, two bottles of sparkling water arrive at the table.

When he returns, he gives his champagne flute to a passing waiter. "Do you want him to take your glass, too?" he asks me. I pass it, half-full, to the waiter. *Way to stop Brett on his re-fill mission.* Drew does the same for Sienna.

When Sienna visits the toilet, a few men watch her. She's attractive, and any guy would be glad to escort her home. *Will Drew?* The thought rattles me so much that I snap at him when he next asks about George, then slug some water and excuse myself.

In the restroom, I wash my face and hide in the cubicle for longer than an acceptable amount of time. When I emerge, the lights in the restaurant are further dimmed, and the piano man is singing *Lean on Me*. It's a song my mother used to over-play in the car; I would tease her for being so sappy, but tonight, I tear up.

Everyone's attention is on the singer as I return to my chair. I dwell on my mother, on the thoughts my father put to paper, and the words I fired off at Drew on George's jetty. It's clear I'm kidding myself, and the possibility of Drew being with Sienna makes me miserable. I'm plain jealous, and I want him to want me—even if I can't have him. *Now I'm acting like Emily.*

When the song finishes, I blink, but there are too many tears and they mob my cheeks. I flick at them before everyone turns back to the table, but I'm too late. Drew's confused expression metamorphoses into worry. He mouths, "You okay?"

Brett slaps an arm across my shoulders, making me jump. "More bubbly? Anyone fancy a sing-song?" Brett whoops and claps. "Who can play the piano?" He resembles a bullet fired in a metal room, forever ricocheting off the walls.

"Come on, Brett," Drew says. "You know you sing like a train whistle."

"That's just cold," he replies, refilling his glass.

Drew's questioning gaze barely leaves my face for the next few minutes. His eyes tug at mine, and the pleasant fluttering sensation returns, which intensifies with each lingering glance. Flustered, I fall back on my distraction technique and ask Sienna a dozen questions about life in England.

"I was studying to be a nurse but fainting at the sight of blood wasn't exactly on the list of qualifications," she explains.

"What are you going to do instead?"

"I don't know. That's why I went traveling. Jeez, this restaurant is amazing, isn't it?" She glances around as if it's Disneyland.

"Drew and I are familiar with every 'must-be-seen-at' restaurant in Sydney," Brett says. "They recognize us on sight, don't they, mate?"

Drew fingers his dessert spoon and simply smiles.

"You look so familiar, Emily." Sienna inspects me through the dim light. "Have you ever visited England?"

I stare ahead, rigid. Sienna might be recalling a news report. "People are always saying that," I say. "I have one of those faces." My voice sounds rusty.

"Where do you live in America?" Sienna persists. "My parents are originally from Cape Cod."

"West Coast." My words are snipped off, willing Sienna to

leave it. Brett takes a sip from his glass. He frowns at me over the rim. I watch the spoon I'm pushing in circles.

"You can clear something up for me actually," Sienna continues. "What's the difference between cyclones, hurricanes, a twister, a tornado—"

"This conversation is tragic." Brett drains his glass and bangs it onto the table. "Jeez, ladies, another subject? I need a piss . . . and a round of butterscotch Schnapps." He scrapes his chair noisily and wobbles away. I wonder if Drew will have something to say about Brett's behavior, but he doesn't. Maybe this is normal.

When Brett returns, he gets louder and louder and puts a possessive hand on my knee. The rowdier he becomes, the more people glance at our table, raising the chances of someone recognizing me.

Murderer.

I hide behind my hair, use my press-on smile. But when Drew and Sienna get up to leave, the air is vacuumed out of my lungs.

"I'll walk Sienna back to the resort," Drew says to no one in particular.

"Yeah, didn't she need a light bulb changing?" Brett shouts. He slugs the Schnapps I didn't touch. "Good one, mate."

My stomach hits the floor.

"'Night, Emily," Sienna says. I give a jerked wave and a taut smile, then cut to Drew but he's giving Brett a dirty look.

"I'll cover the bill," Brett slurs. "You can barely afford toothpaste."

Drew drops some bills onto the table. My throat wrings itself out when he says, "See ya, Emily."

I can only nod. So much for parting on better terms. As Drew and Sienna walk away, Sienna links her arm through

Drew's, and a waiter comes to our table to inform us they're closing.

"I should go anyway, Brett," I say. "I'll get a taxi. What's George's address?"

"Ten more minutes." Brett raises his brandy glass, swilling the brown liquid. After a few more slur-filled minutes, the bar lights flicker off. Brett curses. "A little time here," he barks. "Come. We can finish on the beach."

"You go. I'll—"

"Come on, Gotta Go Girl. We need to walk to Drew's resort to get a taxi anyway." He sways to his feet and tugs at my hand. I pull it away but follow.

A dark part of me imagines Drew kissing Sienna right at that moment.

CHAPTER 13

I trek after Brett down several flights of rickety stairs to the beach. When I flick off my flip-flops, the sand is cool between my toes, but my brain is hot and fuzzy from the belated effects of the champagne. I'm zombie-like as I focus on the lights of the Coconut Palm Beach Resort ahead. Drew will probably spend the night with Sienna. The possibility paints me black.

Brett throws an arm over my shoulders and propels me in the direction of the resort. I push him off, stumbling and exhausted by his constant energy.

"Drew and Sienna got on," he says, an arm once again around my shoulders. I give up objecting, melancholy pushing through me like a drug. "She's a bit . . . shall we call it repressed?" He pauses. "Yes, let's call it repressed."

"She seems very nice."

"Did you see Vega's reaction when *we* walked in?" He slaps his thigh, sniggering.

I twist away and walk backward, facing Brett. "Who did Drew think he was coming on a date with tonight?"

His laugh is surly. He grabs my wrist and seizes my other arm and swoops to steal a kiss.

"Don't." I whip my face to the side. Lightheaded from the alcohol, I pull away and keep walking, quickening my pace.

Except Brett follows and grips my elbow. "Are you teasing me? Is this a 'no means yes' game?" His expression alters from lazy to predatory.

A fat slice of fear wedges into my chest.

"I'm not playing games." I yank at my arm, but his grip is a vice.

His face morphs into a snarl. "Why the mean girl act? You're here. You let me buy you dinner—"

"Only because you wouldn't let me pay—"

"You're a game player. You've got that whole *I don't know how gorgeous I am* thing going on. Do you realize how that can tease a guy? Yeah, you know," he sneers and sways on his feet, mirroring the shadows of the palm trees around us. "That and your mystery, Gotta Go Girl act. Come on, a friendly good night kiss." His words melt together.

"It's not a game or an act." This time, I pull hard enough to free my arm. Brett hurls the brandy glass into the sand, grabs my shoulders, and crashes his lips to mine. His breath smells syrupy and moldy.

I smell Connor and feel the strength and power that will hurt me. Fear flares through my veins as it had that last night with Connor. He had come home early and was drinking while he waited for me. Furious that I'd gone sailing and again accusing me of having an affair with some sailor, he held me against the kitchen wall by my neck, my tiptoes only just skimming the floor. His tongue filled my mouth, further choking me. His hands ripped at my shorts, roughly kneaded my breasts. When my air ran out, stars prickled my vision. I felt myself go limp but was thrown to the ground like his ragdoll. I hit my skull on the tiles and saw lit sparklers behind my eyes before I passed out.

He had left me on the floor in the dark.

I rolled into a ball on my side. My body throbbed with

pain. I lay in my own drool and blood, unable to move. In the lounge, I could hear the clink of ice cubes and Connor playing his old CDs. I listened to the grandfather clock. Each tick stabbed at my brain. He had never hurt me like this before. He controlled every part of my life, yelled, spat, punched, but never this.

Later, Connor called for me in that way that suggested he wanted sex. Apparently, he'd forgotten where he'd left me. His voice angered when I didn't reply. As he crashed toward the kitchen, calling out for his whore, I sat up, stifling a cry of pain, opened the cutlery drawer, and retrieved the carving knife.

But I didn't have a knife now. The fear I had lived with morphs into a pure-white fury as it finally had with Connor. I drop my flip-flops and grit my teeth, grab Brett's forearms, and thrust him away. My fingers barely reach around his biceps, and it's as futile as pushing against a moving car. His right-hand clamps behind my head, the other behind my back. I kick at him, but his legs are tree trunks. I bite his lip.

He jolts backward, blood oozing. He wipes his mouth with the back of one hand while the other still grasps my elbow.

"Seriously. I said *no."* I knee him in the groin but don't quite reach. I become a frenzied rush of arms and legs as I kick and shove. But I have the strength of a fairy compared to him. No matter how strong I am inside, physically, a man is always stronger.

"Brett."

I can't see him, but I know its Drew's voice that distracts Brett enough for me to free an arm.

"Get lost, Vega," Brett shouts.

I punch Brett's left cheek, putting all the anger I've bottled up into that punch. He stumbles back, looking more shocked than hurt, then lunges forward again. I side-step him. A flash of Drew . . . the crunch of flesh on bone stabs the air. Brett topples and lands with a dull thud in the sand.

I am suddenly angry with everyone—my mother for not leaving my dad, my dad for changing into the man he became, Finn for abandoning me, Connor for not being the life raft I needed, Brett for using his strength over me, and even Drew. So, when he approaches, I hold up both hands to warn him off.

"I was handling it," I yell, shaking. "I can fight my own battles." I brace myself, breaths ragged, not truly believing my words. Inside, I'm splintering apart. "I don't need your help just because I'm a girl." My voice is not my own—it's loud and hard and filled with rage.

Why did I have to be born a girl?

And suddenly, I'm pounding my fists against Drew as if he's the one who attacked me. He steps back, but I keep coming.

Disbelief and anger twist through his features. "Don't tell me I should've stood and watched just so you could prove you were handling it," he shouts. "That's not what a guy does in that situation, okay? Especially when I *knew* this would happen."

I draw away from him. "You knew?" *Does Drew blame me?*

Drew spins on the spot, punches his fist into his palm, then kicks at the sand and shakes out his hands, fingers splayed wide. Groaning, Brett rolls onto his side, arms helmeting his head. Drew squats to pat his shoulder, but Brett shrugs him off. Drew stays crouched, staring at his friend for a long time and I feel like flotsam again. I retrieve my flip-flops and, stumbling over my feet, head for the darkened resort. The adrenaline is gone, and my legs now resemble whale blubber.

In the deserted bar, I deposit myself on a sofa and ball up. I hear Drew's trudging footsteps. A few moments pass, and he nudges my arm with a glass of water. Too angry to be mollycoddled, I skid it onto the table, asking myself how it is that I've become some sort of victim. A *nasty-guy* magnet.

Drew paces between the sofa and the bar, pulsing with emotion.

When I can trust myself to speak, I sit up straighter and wind my hair into a makeshift ponytail. "What did you mean when you said you *knew* this would happen? It wasn't my fault." My voice is raspy.

"*No.* I didn't mean that." He strides closer and reaches toward my shoulder, re-thinks, and plunges onto the sofa opposite, elbows on knees. Clasping and unclasping his hands, he stares into space. "It's Brett. *He's* trouble."

"Then why do you travel with him?"

Drew splays his fingers over his face. "Dumping him is giving up on him. Or betrayal. You don't know what he's been through . . . what we've been through. I know he doesn't project it, but inside, he's a broken man. Except, he's getting worse. He used to be a free spirit, then it became more of a loose cannon, but now . . ."

He brushes the light stubble on his chin, still avoiding my stare. "It's as if he has no boundaries, no concept of right and wrong. As if he's losing himself and becoming someone else. He wasn't always like this. I don't know what to do. I can't abandon him. He has no one. Some days, I'm his brother and his parent rolled into one. And they say that a parent always loves their child, no matter what." He examines me, grasping for the precise words. "I know you think I should confront him, but it wouldn't end well. Last time I did, he went missing for over a week, and I found him sleeping rough, passed out in his own piss and vomit. I can't have him go off on his own. He'd end up in the wrong crowd and somehow kill himself. I'd rather be his bodyguard. But I'm sorry you had to—"

"What happened to him? Why has he got nobody but

you?" I recall my father's letter about the monster that lurked inside him. Did Brett have a monster lurking inside him, too?

"It's not my story to tell. But trust me, it's worse than anything you can imagine. And abandoning him would be like kicking a stray injured dog that's just been run over and is barely hanging on to life." Drew glances toward the beach, groans, and holds his face in his hands. "When I returned to the restaurant and you'd gone, I got a bad feeling." He speaks through his fingers. "I shouldn't have left you. I planned to come back, put you in a taxi. I should've taken you with us, but I figured it might wind Brett up." His eyes slide to mine. "And I wanted to talk to you . . . alone."

We lapse into a silence that softens as the minutes pass.

Drew circles his head to release tension from his neck, slumps into the sofa, and runs his fingers through his hair. "Brett needs help. But he reckons shrinks are for wimps. I have tried." He stares at me, bleak. "Remember how I said I didn't want you to bump into him again? That you were a prize to be won. And tonight, he kept pawing you—" He stands, arms rigid at his side, paces again, looking as if he needs to clobber something. "*That's* what I meant when I said I knew this would happen. He was claiming you tonight and sending me a message."

"But he didn't know—we . . ."

"One thing Brett's not, is stupid. He'd seen enough." Drew sits, stands again, paces.

"Has he ever let you have a girlfriend without muscling in?"

"Only if he was involved with someone else at the time. He can be intense, so when he's with a girl, it's all or nothing."

"He came aboard *Sassy*, uninvited," I say. "He suggested dinner with *friends,* and I was so bored and lonely, waiting for George to find parts. I made him swear it wasn't a date."

Drew perches on the sofa again. "He gave me the friends-for-dinner line, too. I guessed he lured you there under false pretences as well, so I let him play his game. What else could I do? I wasn't going to leave you and Sienna there. Besides, I knew you wouldn't want anything to do with him, not if you meant what you said about priorities and getting to Australia."

I wince inside his hurt gaze and swallow the last of my anger. "You've confronted Brett now. How does it feel?"

Elbows on knees, Drew hangs his head again. "I'm not keen on thumping mates I've known all my life. A mate who's been there for me when *I* needed him, like when my mom died . . . and stuff with my dad." He seems to choke on the final word. Then he clears his throat. "*You* were like a demon." He flashes me a look of approval, one that contains warmth and humor and pushes up the heat in my blood a notch. But then he looks away, pinching the bridge of his nose. "And I reckon every bit of frustration and anger I ever felt against Brett boiled up in me when he lunged at you. I put all of it into punching him—that makes me a jerk. He needs help, not a beating."

"Did his father abuse him or something?"

"No. Nothing like that."

"Worse than that?"

When Drew doesn't respond, I stare at the white caps forming on the waves out to sea. The tension trickles from me. "Is he still out there?"

"No. I saw him leave when I poured you that water. He'll have gotten a taxi."

"Did you break his jaw?"

"Doubt it. Possibly his nose." We exhale a silent chuckle, and he watches me, lips twitching as he stills a smile. His tender gaze nudges mine.

Tears jam into my eyes and my mouth twists, not because of Brett, but because everything seems so messed up. Drew gets up, parks himself next to me, and pulls me under his arm.

"You going to be okay?" he whispers.

A sob rises in my throat, and I can only nod against his torso. My hair escapes from its makeshift ponytail, and Drew strokes it in long sweeps down my back. The gentleness of his touch pokes a hole in my armor and all the pent-up emotion of the last two days unspools. I sob inside the circle of his arms, and he holds me until I hush. The ocean crashes rhythmically and we hold each other in silence, as if neither of us knows what else to do, or perhaps, neither of us wants to do anything else.

DREW'S THUMB strokes my cheek. I stir. I had dozed off, and he'd moved my legs across his lap so he could cradle me. We couldn't be closer. I know only one thing—I don't want to be alone on *Sassy* tonight. I can't return to that gut-yanking loneliness of the last two days.

"Don't go back to *Sassy Jam* tonight," he whispers, his breath hot on my ear. I ache to place my hand on his chest, his shoulder, to feel the skin and muscle under his shirt. "I'll be too worried to sleep. You could stay here in the girls' fale."

I pause for only a moment before agreeing.

He adds, "Be okay here for two minutes? I'll call in a favor."

I twist round and remove my legs from his lap and check the clock behind the bar.

Drew stands and looks down at me with bottomless concern. The sharp desire to kiss him lances through me. My breath snags and for a tick in time, Drew's eyes blaze. He hesitates, but turns away, leaving me alone.

Minutes later, he returns with Sienna who, dressed in an oversized T-shirt, is spritely, even at three in the morning.

"Come on, darling. Let's get you tucked in." She urges me up as if I'm a child and sets her arm around my shoulders to guide me out of the bar. "'Night, Drew." Her tone is mock disapproving. "You owe me dinner."

As we pass him, Sienna reaches out to squeeze his bicep, her hand resting there a little too long.

CHAPTER 14

When I wake, I'm alone in the fale. The other beds are empty, their sheets unkempt as if abandoned in a hurry. Vanilla sunlight slides through the wooden slats at the glass-less windows, slants toward the white floor tiles, and pounces onto the pale walls of the circular room. A blanched mosquito net hangs above me, tied in a knot. It lilts in the breeze in time with the other four nets above similar single beds. Even the blankets are white.

It's the first time I've slept in a real bed in over two months. It was dry and soft and stayed still. I sit up and work my fingers through my hair to pull out the knots and scan the bright-blue ocean out the shuttered windows. Not bad digs for travelers working in a hotel.

I switch my thoughts to Drew. My lips tilt up involuntarily. *He came back for me.*

In the ensuite bathroom, I choose toothpaste from a choice of five tubes and brush my teeth with a finger. I intend to find the bar to say hello to Drew, but as I leave, I almost trip over him. He's sitting on the steps of the fale.

"Morning," he says. He's wearing a white vest top and mushroom-colored shorts to his knees and when he stands, we're so unexpectedly close on the little porch step, my bones gloop to jelly. He reaches up to hang his arms from the low fale roof, as if to find something for his hands to do. *Holy muscles.* My breath is caged in my throat.

I step backward into the open doorway. "Morning. And thanks for . . . last night. Are you guarding me?"

"Don't sound so suspicious. I'm simply kidnapping you."

I raise my eyebrows but can't squash down a smile.

"You must be starved," he adds. "You didn't eat much last night." He drops down the three steps in one stride and reaches behind them to fetch a brown paper bag. "Breakfast." Flashing his all-Australian smile, he beckons me to follow.

We stroll to the beach where we settle on the sand. He passes over a cup of something. "Soup made from pawpaw and coconut cream. It's disgusting, but you should try it at least once. Very authentic."

I eyeball it. "Oh, gee thanks."

He laughs, and it turns into an infectious belly laugh as I sip the soup and pull a face. Still chuckling, he exchanges it for the paper bag, which contains a pastry. I hug my knees and munch while he leans back on his forearms, tanned legs stretched in front of him. He reaches for my ankle to trace the shape of the sea eagle tattoo. The tattoo feels like a battle scar. For a moment, I had reclaimed some control of my life. Connor had hated it—that was the first time he hit me. Now, Drew's finger becomes a lightning bolt that sends thousands of volts through my veins.

"You're full of surprises, Emily. Such a closed book, yet you're sailing across the Pacific on your own and—"

"My name's Shae." I can't bear him calling me the name of my roommate a moment longer. "I know. I know. Another lie. But I didn't know you back then."

His finger slips from my ankle, his brow pinches. He pushes himself upright. "And you've kept it up all this time?"

"Sorry."

Drew plays with the sand between his bent knees, a fixed, fake grin in place. "Why didn't you want to tell me your real name? What's in a name?"

I scramble for an answer, reprimanding myself. "Brett reckons I'm a game player. I'm not. I don't intend to be. I'm just not very trusting."

At the mention of Brett, Drew straightens and balls the paper bag. "Brett knows nothing. I prefer Shae anyhow. Suits you." His face exudes warmth as if he's painting me with sunshine. "Anything else you want to tell me though?"

Knowing any hesitation will stamp me with guilt, I say no quickly. *Just that one secret I can't ever tell.*

"Do you like bike riding?" he asks.

"It's only my second favorite thing to do."

He raises an eyebrow and looks as if he's going to ask about my favorite thing but decides not to press. "I'm supposed to visit the village this morning, the one I mentioned that needs a total rebuild. Want to come? It's a fifteen-minute bike ride."

I sit cross-legged and stare out to sea, steeling myself against the delight dancing inside me. "I should get back to *Sassy* and George. He needs my help."

"About that . . . I called George to tell him where you were. He said he's waiting on a part for the windvane, so nothing can be done today."

"You called George?"

Both Drew's hands fly up in surrender. "I wasn't being controlling or bossy before you go off. Figured he'd be worried if he worked out you didn't come home last night, okay?"

I circle my knees with my arms, unable to look at him, my resolve already weakened by picturing myself scrubbing out the bilge, alone for yet another day. "George must think I'm a dirty stop-out." I pop the last of the pastry into my mouth.

"He did mention something about that." I choke on my

mouthful, and Drew claps me on the shoulder. "Would you rather spend time helping out at the village where people need you or be alone on *Sassy* all day? Brett may even pay a visit—I should talk to him before you go back to your boat."

"I'm not afraid of him." Except, I am.

Drew chuckles. "Yeah, I can believe that."

I play-punch his arm and he falls aside, pretending he's mortally wounded.

I run through how Drew stepped in last night and didn't make any moves. He's the good guy. He knows I don't want more than friendship—that I have other priorities. We could be friends just as he and Sienna seem to be. Because anything more will only hurt him. And no one's going to recognize me —we'll be in a derelict village surrounded by Samoans who don't have TV or use Google. It'd be something to do, to pass the time.

When I give him a sideways glance, his face is at ease— such a contrast to the confused and wistful looks he failed to hide the last time I pushed him away. I wrestle with myself, my determination to decline thinning by the second.

"I'll be a friend coming along to help, like Sienna does?" I ask.

His smile becomes wry and he surveys the beach. "Exactly right."

"I'm not quite dressed for building work."

We glance at my white shorts and halter top, and I turn the color of raspberry jam.

"You won't be doing building work. And I can lend you a T-shirt if you don't mind it being small for you." His grin teases, cheeky, *and way too hot.* "Come on. The hotel has hire bikes." He stands and pulls me to my feet. "You should see some of the real Samoa. The people in this village are cool and so un-Westernized. Come and do your bit."

"Put like that, how can I say no?"

CHAPTER 15

Thirty minutes later, I'm pedaling after Drew along a potholed dirt road, his black T-shirt so big on me, I've tied it in the middle. He swerves around fallen palm fronds, pedals fast on smoother ground, and leaps over rocky mounds and ditches. I'm happy he doesn't baby me, and I whoop, steering the bike to vault and catch air. Mountain biking had been a large part of my life before I met Connor, but he hated me doing activities without him so I'd given it up, fighting only for my sailing time.

We dive left down a sandy path with long tangled grass on either side until we emerge onto the beach. The lumpy, dry sand halts his progress, and Drew dismounts. When I copy him, my bike chain jumps off its cog. I lift it into place, pull up the back wheel, and spin it. The chain slots back into gear.

Drew raises a hand for a high-five. "Nicely done."

I slap his hand, but he doesn't move on. His gaze swallows me whole.

"What?" I ask.

"Why were you crying last night when you came back from a visit to the toilet that was so long, I figured you'd done a runner out the window?" His smile is tinged with concern. "And I won't accept a shrug for an answer."

"That song. It reminded me of my mom."

"You're homesick?"

I shrug.

He bumps the back wheel of his bike into the front wheel of mine, then passes me a bottle of water from his backpack.

When we reach the wet packed sand, Drew takes off again, hurtling along the shoreline and spraying seawater as he pulls up into wheelies. I shadow his moves, even overtake him, welcoming the sprinkler effect on my hot skin. We hit another dirt road, race down a steep incline, hurdle fallen branches, skid around larger ones, and confirm we're both speed junkies. Drew hockey stops, spinning a three-sixty. I skid side-on and splatter his legs with stones and dust. He whacks me on the back as if I passed an initiation test.

"You're mental," he says.

Puffing hard, our eyes smash together. I don't look away. He makes me feel like Superwoman.

Catching our breath, we push our bikes up a short road.

"Ten thousand homes got decimated after the cyclone last year," Drew says. "The rebuilding will take years. This village had no safe drinking water, no toilets, no electricity. They're only now getting back on their feet, although many of them are still living ten people to one small room." He leans his bike against a tree trunk and props mine against his. "When I first came here, the house over there had a whole car lodged in its wall." He points to a roofless, derelict home.

The village is more of a dilapidated waste ground—metal roof sheeting tossed like paper into random piles, wooden beams that were once part of someone's home slung in spiky heaps. The remaining homes resemble broken doll houses with tarpaulins as roofs. A couple of steel-framed beds protrude from under a pile of rubble, and palm trees have been sliced in half while banana trees lay almost flat on the ground.

"It's as if I'm walking into a news story on *CNN*," I say.

Drew ambles beside me, carrying his backpack. Our arms swing side by side. "We lost our breadfruit trees—one of their incomes apart from fishing. And four people lost their lives, including a young couple who married the week before." He turns to me, his stare barbed. I suspect he's making a point about me setting sail when cyclone season's about to start.

"The Disaster Management Office can't keep up, so they're relying on volunteers."

"Like you."

"And Sienna. She brought me here when I arrived."

We walk past another house, its rusty sheet metal walls warped. I peer through a gap and detect a boy of about eight perched on a table in the middle of the one-roomed home. It's the only piece of furniture there.

Ahead, in the center of the village, women wash clothes in huge wooden tubs, and men carry long logs back and forth. As we emerge into the opening, a couple of children shriek, "Meester Drew. Meester Drew." They run to him and pull at his shirt.

"Talofa," Drew responds, ruffling their hair.

Within moments, more children come running, some holding pieces of paper that flap in the breeze. They thrust pencils at him, shouting, "Fa-aah-moly-moly," in high-pitched voices, their white teeth flashing inside dark faces.

"Later. Later," he says, laughing when they tug at his arms. An adult shouts something, and the children step back from Drew, still chattering. More adults congregate to see what the commotion is.

"What do they want?" I ask.

"They want me to draw for them." The children's attention swings to me, and their high-pitched voices babble at

Drew again. "O le ma tama teine," he replies, stumbling through the sounds. The adults of the village burst into raucous laughter, the men slapping their knees and each other's backs. Drew chuckles. "Apparently, I just told them you're our daughter."

"Matagofie," a small boy shouts. A ripple of giggles and whispers run through the gathering group.

"He says you're beautiful," Drew explains, his lips twitching.

"Thank you," I say to the child, not even hiding behind my hair. "Drew, where did they get the paper and pencils from?"

"I leave it for them." He high-fives one of the younger boys.

The children are ushered away by a Samoan man dressed in jeans and a brown shirt that hangs open because it's lost every button. He grips Drew's handshake with both hands. "Afio mai, Mr. Drew. We are building Tupa's house today," the Samoan says. He studies me for a moment. "I see you've brought us more help."

"This is Shae. She's visiting Samoa."

The man surveys a group of women behind him. "Pika," he shouts, beckoning. A large woman in a sky-blue T-shirt and what appears to be a green tablecloth wrapped around her waist as a skirt tramps toward us. The man gives her a respectful nod, then says something to her, and she shyly indicates for me to follow. I glance at Drew as I walk away, and he's still tracking me when I look up again a moment later.

I'm hanging wet clothes on a makeshift washing line between two broken-in-half homes, listening to the women babble and giggle amongst themselves, when Drew comes into sight. He's transporting a thick log with two other men, hoisted on their shoulders as if carrying a coffin. Next, he climbs the wooden frame of a home, hauling a bucket of tools as he works alongside several others who wear yellow plastic safety vests.

I help the women fill huge woven baskets with coconuts and breadfruit, and we lug them back to the village. When the men come for a break, they rest on fallen logs and accept wooden bowls of water to drink and mango to eat. Drew scarfs the food down, his T-shirt sticking to him in the heat. The women take their own fruit and settle on the ground, chattering.

As I finish my water, Drew drops into the gap between me and another woman. Our knees overlap when he squats. "You okay? Surviving?" he asks.

"Yes. It's an amazing experience. To see this . . . Everyone's so happy." I gesture at the people. "It's humbling."

The other men prepare to leave, and Drew pushes to his feet. "They appreciate your help." I half-hope he'll kiss my cheek or squeeze my hand before he leaves. Instead, he says, "Nice shirt."

I tell myself I'm pleased Drew's keeping to 'just friends,' but I'm left longing for the sight of him the rest of the morning.

Three women indicate for me to follow. We fold stiff tarpaulin and carry it to a dry hut to store between rows of makeshift beds. Later, when I return to the center of the village, Drew is sitting in the middle of a circle of children, his head bent low as he concentrates on the strokes of his pencil. He passes the drawing to a child who runs to show his mother. The remaining children prod Drew with flapping pieces of paper. They observe, slack-jawed, as if he's creating magic on the page.

I watch his strong, sure hands work, remembering how they'd gently cared for the stray dog. I want to stay here with Drew, get to know him—know him always. And it's a deep need, like needing to eat or sleep, rather than just desire. What would it be like to be with someone who is tender and loving? Someone who draws and bike rides and understands my love of sailing.

I'm still staring into space when something pings my cheek.

"Always loved spit balls," Drew says. "Come sit with us." He asks a child to make some room. I step between the squatting children and plonk beside Drew. He keeps drawing, this one a parrot. Some of the children reach to stroke my arm and hair.

"They're fascinated by the color of your skin and hair," he says. Between pencil strokes, he casts a sideways glance that is both tender and cheeky. "I know the feeling."

My heart squeezes. An aching heat floods into my groin.

Drew delivers the parrot drawing to a child and accepts another piece of blank paper. The movement of the pencil is quick, certain, and I can understand why they think it's thrilling as the shape of a tiger magically appears on the page.

A white van rattles into the village, breaking hard to avoid the children who race toward it. I'm amazed to see Sienna hop out. The children go crazy, leaving Drew's magic circle to greet her.

"She brings lollies," Drew explains. Sure enough, the children surround us again, each sucking on honey-scented boiled candy. They don't throw away the colorful wrappers, but flatten them on their legs, chattering and admiring each one. "She's probably brought in supplies." He doesn't look up as he works on a rooster drawing.

"I'll help unload." I get up and step through the children.

Sienna sees me, then scans the area until she spies Drew. "Emily. How are you after last night?"

Not knowing what Drew told her, I say, "Fine, thanks. Thanks for the bed. I hope you got to sleep again."

Sienna doesn't reply, but walks round the back of the van, flinging open the double doors. A group of women gather behind her, waiting to help. Sienna passes out boxes labeled *mosquito coils, water purification tablets,* and *first aid.* We stack them in the same hut as the tarpaulin until Drew comes over.

"Hey, Sienna," he says.

Her face brightens when she greets him back, and she smooths down her pale-blue T-shirt. *What exactly is their history? Or future?* The possibility of the two of them getting together after I leave hurts so much more than it should.

"I brought Shae to help this morning," Drew adds.

Sienna stares at me. "Shae?"

I break into a sweat and wipe my upper lip.

Drew steps in front of me. "A nickname. She reminds me of someone."

Sienna scrunches her face. "You're weird." She looks from him to me, and back again. "You two are inseparable." Her voice is colorless.

"Just showing Emily the sights," he explains.

"The inside of a vet clinic and a half-destroyed village? Nice tour guide, Drew." Sienna play-punches his arm, and he bends to pick up a small branch, chucks it on a pile of rubble. She turns back to me. "You still look so familiar, Emily. Have you been on TV?" Sienna's stare fixes on me.

Why did I reveal my real name? Hearing it might trigger a memory. Or if Sienna sees a news story, she'll bust me. Sienna is clearly head-over-heels keen on Drew, so ratting on me would clear the way for her. She'd excuse it as her civic duty. I killed someone, after all.

I must get off this island.

"What's your last name?" Sienna asks.

I can't not answer. "Ah . . . Stern." The sun pulses on my skin. I fan myself with my hand.

"Same as the front of a boat. That's a coincidence."

"Back of a boat," Drew jumps in.

"And when are you leaving for Australia? What's your boat called?"

Too many questions. Sienna knows something. I can't reveal

117

Sassy's name because it's too memorable. Silence hangs over the three of us, a loaded gun. Drew stares into the treetops, looking like he swallowed something too hot.

"I'm not sure when I'm leaving," I finally say. "Soon."

"Jeez, Sienna," Drew butts in, "you're a one-woman interview panel."

Sienna withers beside me. No one speaks, and we stare at the villagers who have gathered to eat lunch.

"I have to drive back for my shift. Do you need a lift?" Sienna asks, looking at Drew from under her lashes.

"Thanks. But we came on bikes. We've been earning our lunch, too." He points at two bowls of food waiting on a tree stump. "Guess we'll see you later."

Not if I can help it. The less I see of Sienna, the less she'll try to figure out why she recognizes me.

Drew and I watch Sienna jump into the van. Our arms touch. Drew looks down at me. *Oh so close.* If I tiptoed, our lips would meet. His eyes rake across my face. "So, *were* you on TV?"

A dog trots toward us, and I bend to stroke it, then straighten, shaking my head.

"I'm starved," Drew says, shoulder bumping me and heading for the tree stump.

With his touch, I turn to rice paper fluttering in the breeze.

CHAPTER 16

After lunch, Drew and I wave goodbye to the villagers and wander back to our bikes. When we reach the beach, Drew drops his bike onto the sand and leans over to squeeze my front tire, checking the pressure.

"You okay?" he asks, his face close—within kissing distance. He checks the back tire, his shoulder brushing mine.

My breath hitches. I return his gaze which heats up. But he moves away to fetch his bike, pushing down a grin. I decide he's testing me after what I said about a holiday romance. Teasing me. Or simply taking me at my word and fighting his own feelings.

For the millionth time, my brain has a fistfight with my heart.

Drew takes off in the opposite direction of the resort.

"Where are you going?" I yell, but he's already twenty meters ahead.

The beach is deserted, and I race after him, riding through the shallows to cool down. When he reaches an outcrop of rocks, he jumps off his bike and turns to wait. He raises an approving eyebrow as I hockey-stop and dismount in one movement.

"This isn't the way back," I say, out of breath.

"I always go for a swim to cool off after hard labor. The rock pool's through there." He jerks his chin toward the trees. "The tours visit in the mornings, but they move off after lunch." I squint at him, wary, but then follow, leaping barefooted across the rocks and feeling light on my feet because I realize I trust him.

The rocks bleed into rainforest, and I hear the waterfall before I see it. We traipse along a narrow, earthy path through the trees and into a clearing. It's like being at the bottom of a hollow volcano—circular walls are crowded by vines and tropical plants, while mossy curtains hang to complete the effect of having gone back in time to the Jurassic era. At its center is an azure-blue swimming hole that could be in a holiday brochure. Reaching from the pool, against a wall overgrown with plants, is a man-made ladder that must be twenty meters tall.

On the opposite side, a cascading waterfall charges into the pool, so high it's impossible to see the top, as if the water's falling out of a hole in the sky. I stare in awe, turning in circles.

"The tourists know it as The Trench," Drew says, "but the locals call it Eden."

He drops his flip-flops and backpack on one of the giant boulders that circle the pool, whips off his T-shirt, and bombs into the water. Feeling dusty and sticky with sweat, I strip to my black bikini and dive in after him. When I surface, Drew is treading water in front of me. The air around us pulses with life, heavy with trapped heat and the perfume of the rainforest.

"We're supposed to climb that ladder and jump," he shouts over the roar of the falls. "You game?"

"Race you," I say. We swim to the ladder. Feeling like I'm

climbing Jack's beanstalk into the clouds, I lose count at twenty-nine rungs. At the top, Drew tells me to step onto the ledge. He follows. We stare into the unusually blue pool about sixty feet below.

"Fling yourself away from the rock edge. It's deep. You won't hit the bottom."

I recall *Sassy* surfing forty-foot waves and decide this is nothing.

"Together?" he asks.

I grab his hand. And jump.

We drop through the air, pulpy vegetation and sky rushing past our vision. When we hit the water, our hands force apart, and our bodies dart like torpedoes through a zillion bubbles. We emerge, laughing and gasping. Drew points to the waterfall. I follow him across the pool and through the tumbling falls where we perch on the rocks behind. The powerful, blaring surge of water wakens every sense, making me feel vibrant and alive. It's as if I've spent the last two months tying myself in knots and stretching myself thin, an elastic band at breaking point, and now Drew is unraveling the knots and slackening the elastic.

It's too noisy to talk so we sit in silence but with crazy grins on our faces. I run my hands over slicked-back wet hair and ring it out. Drew watches me. The air in my lungs stutters. I rest my head against the rock face. Moments later, there's a loud splash. Drew floats toward the edge of the pool and settles onto one of the huge rocks to sunbathe. When I lie on my belly next to him, he turns to me and smiles.

"I've got something for you," he says, then sits and rummages through his backpack. He passes me a piece of folded paper.

It's a pencil sketch of me. In it, my hair is stupidly long, and my mouth is soft and serious. Mostly, he's captured a sadness behind my eyes. *My secret.*

"It's . . .Well, it's of me so I can't say it's beautiful, but you're very talented." I blush to my core and re-fold the drawing. "Thank you. Keep it safe for me?"

He stows it, and I twist my hair into a side braid. Drew lobs a bottle of lotion at me, and we apply sunscreen while talking about the first time I helmed a boat on my seventh birthday.

"Lie down, and I'll do your back," Drew says.

My breath clutches.

I lie on the hot rock as he kneels beside me and rubs his palms together to warm the cream. I lock my focus on the pool ahead, chin resting on my arms. He smooths the lotion into my shoulders, his pace ultra-slow. Certain he's lingering and teasing, I suppress a giggle but struggle to control my breathing when he skims his hand under the bikini strap across my back. He strokes farther into the small of my spine, and I bite down a gasp when the tips of his fingers brush the fabric of my bikini bottoms. His fingers are a match, and he's lit a fire inside me.

Deciding that's enough, I bounce onto my knees. "Your turn."

He passes the bottle then lies flat on the rock. Possibly to fill the loaded silence or to punish him for his slow teasing, I pump three cold splats of sunscreen across his back until he shouts out, arching and laughing. He twists toward me and narrows his eyes in mock anger. "I'll have to get you back for that, *Shae*."

Although I rub in the lotion quickly, it's impossible to ignore the firmness of his wide shoulders or the shape of his back muscles as they give way to his narrow waist.

After a while, I say, "I'm sorry you had to lie to Sienna . . . about my name."

He tenses but keeps his focus on the ladder.

"Did you hear me?" I ask.

He lifts onto his elbows, still staring ahead. "I heard you.

Don't worry about it." He flicks a stone into the water. "So, Shae Stern, huh?"

Another lie. "Have you and Sienna been involved?"

He snaps around to face me. "Never." His voice doesn't waver. "We're friends. That's it."

"How come? She's clearly into you."

"Maybe." He squints into the pool and I lie next to him, two lizards belly-down on a rock in the sun. "But there's nothing between us."

"She's cute though?" I rest my cheek on my hand, watching Drew's reaction.

"You trying to hook me up with her?" He copies me, placing his cheek on his hand, his elbow almost touching mine.

"No. Only curious why you're not into her."

His gaze washes over me, thrills me, turns me inside out. He places a finger on my lips as if to hush me. "Because she's not you."

Deep inside me, something cracks wide open.

Feelings I never knew existed escape and shiver through me. My lips part, suck in a breath. His finger plucks my bottom lip and the desire to kiss him, *really kiss him*, leaps from my core.

Drew suddenly stands and in one bound, dives into the pool.

I regain control of my breathing, understanding that he moved away because he thinks I want that.

He returns to sit next to me, arms circling his bent legs. This time, when our eyes find each other, the moment binds us as if we've shared an unfathomable secret.

We exchange growing up tales—how I put whole raw eggs inside my brother's pillowcase before bedtime and how Drew broke his arm when he jumped off a wall, sure he could fly, and why he chose the university in Melbourne to put some distance between him and his father.

"What exactly does your dad do?" I ask.

Drew lies on his stomach before he answers, "He has dollar coins rather than blood flowing through his veins. Had his own trading desk by the age of twenty-five. Went into banking, real estate, IT. My mother was also very career focused."

"At least they weren't lazy asses."

"But they went too far the other way. They lived to work. After my mother died, my father *slept* at the office. If I ever have children, they won't be an only child, and I won't expect them to be a copy of me. And I'll spend time with them. Lots of time. I won't make them feel unimportant or unwanted." Drew flips onto his back and frowns into the circle of sky above our water hole like he's deciphering a message in the flimsy clouds.

"How did your mother die? Is that okay to ask?"

"It was suicide." His words are monotone.

"Oh. Wow. That's hard." I sit cross-legged, watching him. "I'm so sorry." I think about how Brett's mom left him and in a more tragic way, Drew's mom left him, too. Or that's how it might seem to a teenage Drew. No wonder he and Brett are so tight. "Brett said your dad wanted you home by—"

"Let him disown me. I'll be a qualified vet in a few years." Drew's body contracts and an arrow of anger shoots from his eyes into the sky. "There's nothing more to say."

I want to reach out and comfort him. "Did you and your dad get on better when you were younger?"

"We could never talk without it becoming a major confrontation. So, I stayed clear of him. I had to grow up fast. He had me home-schooled from the time my mother died. I was lonely. That's when I discovered drawing. It saved me."

For the first time, I comprehend how Drew relied on Brett's friendship. I wonder what happened to Brett that was so bad, though.

Drew reaches for his backpack and passes me a bottle of sun-warmed water. "One last dip before we go?"

We scale the ladder again but jump one after the other. When I emerge, Drew duck-dives, and I follow. We swim deep into the pool until he turns, and we hang, treading water, facing each other. He reaches to unravel my hair from its braid. As his fingers work to loosen it, his watery gaze never leaves mine—it roams across my face, and the back of his fingers brush my cheek, my lips.

We suddenly need oxygen and kick to the surface.

Sucking in fresh air, Drew gives me a face-splitting grin, laces his fingers through mine, then releases them and dives again. I sink underwater too and, with my hair splayed around my shoulders, swim beside him like we're the people of Atlantis.

I never want the day to end. But behind us, the sun slumps in the sky, a shimmering gold coin resting on the darkened, jagged hills.

AFTER WE RETURN the bikes to the Coconut Palm Beach Resort, Drew takes my hand as if it's the most normal thing in the world. My brain becomes candy floss and doubts dissolve.

We wander along the beach, leaving behind a trail of footprints under an apricot sky. Our shadows mingle with the long silhouettes of the palm trees, and our conversation ambles as the sun dips and sends out the last slivers of daylight.

"Tired?" Drew asks. He lingers on me, checking.

"Nope. Starved though."

"There's a bar we could grab a bite from. It's close."

At the part of the beach where the rainforest reaches the sand dunes, Drew points to a sign hanging from an archway in the trees. The Sandy Grotto is a wooden structure built on high stilts among the foliage of the rainforest. We climb two flights of narrow stairs.

"It's like a hip treehouse," I say.

We're standing on a man-made platform in the rainforest, with only low barriers to stop anyone from falling over the edge and no roof except the canopy. It's packed with young travelers. Most of them nurse cocktails so bright and color-ful, they could rival the parrots that perch in the branches. Music pulses in the background and fairy lights glimmer as night takes hold.

"My turn." I make my way through the crowded bar area. *I probably shouldn't be here.* "What do you fancy? A beer?"

Drew nods and stands close, almost touching.

Someone's written the cocktail list in multi-colored chalk on blackboards propped behind rows of gleaming bottles.

"What was it you mixed for me at Coconut Palms?" I lean into him a little.

"Virgin Pina Colada," he whispers, his chin on my shoul-der. Then he puts his arms around my waist so I'm aware of the warm contours of his chest pressed against my back. A wave of heat stirs in the deepest part of me.

And there's no going back.

We huddle all evening, our knees touching under the table, eyes milking each other. Drew is quick-witted and has me laughing like a child at a pantomime. The real world recedes.

We're the last people to leave.

On the beach, Drew swings an arm across my shoulders, drawing me close. My arm has nowhere else to go but around his waist. When I touch his hipbone, I'm both rattled by and sucked into the intimacy. I know I shouldn't, but I can't pull away. *I'm in too deep.*

"Has to be around midnight," Drew says when we reach the resort.

"I can't believe it. Can I get a taxi at this time of night?"

"With some difficulty. But I have a better idea . . . Wait here."

He mounts the beach stairs two at a time and returns a few minutes later carrying blankets and wearing a different shirt—blue and white checked, the buttons undone. He spreads a blanket and points to the glittering sky. "As the saying goes, we don't need five-star when we have five billion of our own."

I bite my bottom lip, let my hair fall across my face. He's suddenly in front of me, his body so close my chest flickers as if there are a thousand tiny fish swishing their tails in there. He pushes my hair behind my ears and gently holds my face with both hands. My limbs become flowing silk in the breeze, too weak to pull away.

"I'll just keep you warm and safe," he murmurs.

A tremble criss-crosses through me. I blink rapidly. He chuckles and rests his open palms on my hips. My glance scuttles back to his.

"Fearless Shae," he says. "Except so terrified to trust me or to let me in." His gaze delves into mine before his lips brush my mouth. I don't want to pull away. He brushes them a second time before lingering in the softest of kisses, like my lips are as delicate as a daydream and might disappear if he presses too hard.

Every filament of me tingles, the beach tips up, the stars whirlpool.

When he moves away, it's as if I've lost a crutch.

He throws me a clean white T-shirt which I exchange for the black one I borrowed that morning, then I sit on the blanket next to Drew. He puts an arm around me before lying down. My head in the crook of his shoulder, he strokes my hair, pulls my bent leg over his. Our bodies fit like the yin and yang symbol. My insides turn to milkshake. I breathe in the coconut scent of him, concentrating on the sensation of my cheek against his skin. He kisses my temple.

"Shae," he whispers, it seems to himself. The muscles of his shoulder slacken beneath my cheek, and the hand that stroked my hair lies heavy on my hip.

Before I can stop myself, I lift onto my elbow and press my lips to his. Drew opens his eyes, and his lips smile under mine. He rolls me so we're facing each other, and the heat in his expression encourages me to kiss him again. This time, I open my mouth to him, and he slides his tongue between my teeth. I cling to him, pulling him closer, deepening our kiss. I'm inside a new body, one that glows and simmers, whose blood whisks through veins like a summer wind, and whose senses are amplified. Doubt is shoved into the shadows. I want this more than I want to run.

When I feel him hard against me, I hook my leg and use it to clasp his hips closer. I've never felt so sensual, so carnal. Open to a man. He waits for me, rather than leads or pushes. And it's a huge turn on. I feel myself become wetter and gasp into his mouth as his hands wander over the mound of my breast, then to my hips, and down my cocked thigh. His fingertips skim over my bikini between my legs, and I know he can feel how wet I am through the skimpy material.

He slips his fingers inside the bikini, then groans when he feels my slickness. I push myself against his hand, and he rolls me onto my back, freeing his arm to play with me. He pulls at the bow on my bikini so it drops away, and he delves his fingers deep inside me. I arch my back and grab his mouth with mine.

You're leaving Samoa in a few days. You're going to prison for the rest of your life. This is selfish.

The thought is ice thrown over me.

It's all I can do not to sit up and push him away.

Drew must notice a change in me because he withdraws and looks up.

I make myself smile. "Drew . . . just . . . Not here. Not tonight."

He blinks, but then kisses me again, soft, innocent, lowering the heat. Then he gathers me to him, rolls onto his back, and brings me with him. He reaches for another blanket folded to the side and throws it over us, though the night is warm.

"Sweet dreams," he says sleepily.

I'm hollowed out and aching for him. Left with only the sound of his bumping heart beneath my cheek, there's no part of me that wants to sleep, to miss this tender moment. I focus on every inch of me that's touching him. My fingers trace across his moonlit chest, coiling my fingertips in the smattering of hair there. His eyes remaining closed, he places his hand over mine, draws my fingers to his mouth, and kisses their tips. Then he lays my hand back on his chest, his own still cupping it. I imagine drawing his hand between my legs again and how it would feel to make love to him, but it wouldn't be right to give him any ideas that we have a future.

CHAPTER 17

George is humming and tinkering with *Sassy's* engine when I walk down the jetty at seven-thirty. The early morning sun shrouds *Sassy* in a dreamy yellow.

"Ay, ay, my little sirène. Where've you been? I was here at six a.m." His pipe bobs between his lips as he speaks.

"I'm sorry. I was with a friend." My cheeks turn fiery.

"For *two* nights?" He winks. "That good lookin' one, Drew, no doubt?"

"Are you checking up on me, father dear?"

He pokes his pipe at me. "While you're on my jetty, I get to watch ou' for you."

"Sirène? As in siren?" I ask.

"As in French for mermaid. I'm a quarter French, you know. *Now.* See the windvane's nearly fixed, a bit of fine-tuning to do before you can test it, and the lifelines are good as new."

"You're awesome, George." I bound over to hug him.

"Blimey, child. It's a windvane, not a miracle." He pulls back. "Anyhow, it's this damned engine that's giving me gip. I go' the part we need, but it keeps cutting out."

"Is there anything I can do?"

"Not yet. Help yourself to a shower at my place." He tosses the hammer and catches it, resembling a cowboy showing off his gun skills. "And another thing . . . Don't let that boyfriend of yours turn your head. You gotta get ou' of here before a cyclone finds you. I've been watchin' the long-term forecast. Doesn't look good. Check the internet if you want—make yourself at home." He indicates toward his cottage.

I feel like a naughty child. I have thought about leaving, but for the last two days, more in the don't-want-to-leave sense than the practicalities of what I need to do. And here's George, worrying and working on my boat.

In the cabin, I'm like Cinderella after the ball, returning to my old, unmagical life. I pull out the drawing Drew gave me, wishing I had more time to say goodbye this morning. Anton had found us, entwined together in the milkshake light, and totally lost it with Drew for sleeping on the beach—it was like watching a robot blow its own circuits. Apparently, it's *utterly* against hotel policy and *was he aware* the breakfast shift started in twenty minutes. Cracking up and feeling like hooligans, we made a quick exit with no more than a lingering kiss when Drew put me into a taxi. His smile luminous, he waved, then pelted inside to transform into barista man instead of cocktail man.

I trace the pencil strokes on his drawing, remembering how my cheek felt against his chest. How will I say goodbye to Drew, knowing it's probably the last time I'll ever see him?

Maybe I could stay just a couple of weeks longer.

Jeez, he's melting my brain as well as my heart. *Is this what turning into Play-Doh feels like?* I *must* get focused again—not only could the police be closing in on me while *Sassy* is being repaired, but cyclone season is chasing me down. Yet under the shower in George's cottage, I can't stop my mind from walking through yesterday, causing pleasant mayhem to break out inside me.

DREW IS busy with the breakfast shift at the resort today, and then a stint at the dog shelter. After that, he's going to check on Brett. I hope their conversation isn't too difficult. I had told Drew not to worry about me as I had to work on *Sassy*.

"Am I competing with a boat for your attention?" he had asked, only half-joking.

"*Sassy* saved my life more than once. So yes, you probably are."

I recall what I said to Emily many years ago, about rather cuddling a boat than a guy. I'm not quite so sure now.

On the way out of the cottage, George's computer catches my eye. I ought to check the weather forecast, but also the news to assess if the police are any closer. I move the mouse to wake the system, and while it hums and flickers on, I study the portrait of the girl on the pebble beach again. When the computer comes to life, it displays an image that delivers a blow between my eyes. Hot nerves sprawl through me.

George knows.

My heart pinballing in my ribcage, I stare at the photo of myself and the headline:

Reward offered in the search for Shae Love.
The family of Connor Stratton has offered a reward of $1,000,000 for any information that leads to finding 23-year-old Shae Love.

My brain unlatches.

I rush to the window and search in every direction in case George called the police while I was taking a shower. He's still bent over the engine. The sky, ocean, and sand loom and thrust reality into my gut like a wrecking ball. I must leave today. Would George sell me out for that kind of money? It's time to find Uncle Brody and face up to the crime I committed. It's time to deliver my father's letters.

And it's time to leave Drew, probably forever.

As I shut down the page, another thought hits me. George intended for me to see that screen . . . why else would he offer for me to use his computer? And George is so unbothered about money—he hasn't asked me for a dollar yet.

You barely know him.

Through calming breaths, my gut delivers an unexpected answer—I trust George. He's simply giving me a subtle warning to get going. If he's seen the story, then so could others—Brett, Sienna, Vic, *Drew.*

Still shaky inside, I fake a relaxed stroll down the jetty. "How's she doing?" My voice is thin.

George stops humming. "Good, sirène. Almost there." He rifles through deep pockets for some gadget. Did he give me a nickname because he knows my name's not Emily? I check his face for a clue, but he doubles over the engine. I hang my towel on a line and slide below to dump my shower kit.

"Now flick that ignition, would you?" George yells a few minutes later.

I do as he asks and the motor kicks into action. George whoops and performs a jig, and I race on deck to join in with a high-five. He doesn't have the air of a man who's about to betray me.

"Dammit. I've got an extra shift at the surf school," George says. "Tell you what, give the motor a run round here today and when I get back, I've got one thing to fix on the windvane. There's a bolt that needs replacing. I'll fetch it today. Then you can take her for a sunset sail test run. I'll be back at roughly four o' clock. Done?"

"Thanks so much, George. By the way, I keep meaning to ask about the portrait in your lounge. She's beautiful."

George's eyes grow vague and shiny. "Fiona. My daughter. She'd be twenty-three now . . . had she lived."

"I'm sorry. I didn't mean to—"

"S'okay. You'd have got on. She was a sailor, too. I still cry like a lost puppy some days. Been five years." George re-stuffs his pockets and sniffs. It doesn't seem right to ask how his daughter died. "Anyhow," he adds, "you could make sail by tomorrow so get busy, sirène." He gives a clipped, broody wave and lopes up the jetty.

Tomorrow?

I must take my pulsing, exploding, yearning heart and chuck it overboard like an anchor. Yesterday was a moment in time. A great memory, but that's it. *Focus.*

I work through the list of jobs, cleaning winches, removing salt crystals from the solar panels, checking charts, testing the motor. Yet an uneasiness builds in me with each passing minute. Who else might've seen that news story? Every sound has me leaping to inspect it—a car that drives near but keeps going, a squawking parrot, another car, a falling palm frond. Each time, my pulse zips. If George has worked out who I am, so could others, and they might be perfectly happy to collect that reward.

Drew will find out the truth and hate me for lying. He'll hate me for what I did to Connor. No one has the right to take a life. Why didn't I just leave him?

At first, I'd made excuses for his controlling behavior. I thought it was part of the depth of love he felt for me. I was flattered. But when the hitting started, why had I thought I still loved him and he me? I realize now that what I'd felt wasn't love but need. Why had I thought no one else would want me? Why was I ashamed, as if it was *my* fault? I recognize my mother had felt the same way and that's why she denied what my father did. It seems we both let ourselves become isolated and a diminished version of ourselves. I search for some way to understand why I didn't just walk away, but it's like wrestling with an open umbrella in a gale.

Even living on the streets would've been a better option than murder.

Drew will never forgive me for leading him on, knowing that I'm facing life in prison. I let things go too far, spent too much time with him, gave him false hope. *Exactly what I vowed not to do.* I am a bad person, a selfish woman—just like Connor always said.

With my throat plump with emotion, I picture Drew's face when he finds out the truth, and I hope I'm not there to see it.

At four, dressed in my usual shorts and bikini top ensemble, both white today, I pace around *Sassy* and wait for George. He's often on island time. Apart from the windvane, *Sassy* is ready for the final leg of our odyssey. Twenty minutes later, the sound of tires on gravel makes my pulse gallop. I tell myself it's just George.

But it's not.

CHAPTER 18

Out of the long afternoon silhouette cast by George's cottage, Drew materializes. He's smiling as he advances down the jetty, his gaze burrowing into me. My brain empties. The pull to go to him is tidal. It's probably for the last time anyway. My body does all the talking. I jump the gap to the jetty and run to him. He dumps the bag he's carrying and when I bowl into him, he lifts me off the ground. His laugh is an uplifting song.

"You don't mind me swinging by?" he says into my neck.

"Of course not."

Happiness rushes into his face. It's an amazing feeling to realize I do that to him—that I make someone happy. He clasps me tighter, lowers his mouth to kiss me. My body deliciously concertinas into itself and my world shrinks to just the jetty, just us, just his mouth. After years of my family falling apart, of pushing everyone away to keep my secrets, how did Drew blast into my heart?

He puts me down and we stand, holding each other's arms.

"Figured I'd swing by in case you were about to leave," he

says. "George said you're nearly ready." A riot of hurt and confusion criss-crosses his features.

Reality bites, and the thought of leaving topples me. "I wouldn't have gone without saying goodbye."

He blinks dark shadows from his eyes.

"Hi yup. Couldn't stay away?" George's voice makes me jump. He and Drew laugh at my jitteriness.

I cover by nudging the bag at Drew's feet. "Not that soup again."

"Nope. This time it's pig's eyes." His grin, just for me, seems to lift me clear off the deck.

I'm out of control.

Drew picks up the bag. "But if you don't fancy pig's eyes, there's lobster."

"So," George breaks in, "*Sassy's* almost ready. I'm a born natural at this. You can pat me on the back righ' here." He points between his shoulder blades. Drew and I rap him on the back. After a slight pause, George offers a thin grin, jumps onto *Sassy*, and fiddles with the windvane. He remains uncharacteristically silent, not even a hum or a whistle.

My pulse is galloping as I survey the jetty and house behind us.

Drew rubs my arm. "You okay?" His clinging gray T-shirt perfectly outlines his torso.

I push a smile onto my lips. "I have to take her for a sail to test the windvane."

"Can I pay for my passage with lobster?"

I can't say no.

We perch on the gunwale, and Drew chats to George while I scrutinize George's every word. He's not himself. He seems distracted. After a while, George fills his pockets with random tools, but his hands are shaking as if he's rushing or nervous.

"She's ready to go." George straightens, lips pursed, his

expression reflective. All I can think is how I never thought I'd dread hearing those words. "Now don't hang abou', girl. Time's a-marching." Is he referring to the police search or cyclone season? "All you need is more diesel. You can pick tha' up first thing tomorrow. How are you going for food and water?"

"Could do with some fresh fruit and veg." We quieten and scan *Sassy*. "George, thanks. I don't know how—"

"It was a pleasure. Every moment." The look he gives me is tinged with gruff fondness. "Now get ou' of here."

"I have to pay you." I move to the companionway.

"No. Don't worry. I'm good."

"But I want to pay you properly."

He rubs his stubble, slow and deliberate, then glances at Drew, who is still sitting on the gunwale, before stepping closer. "I don't need it. But you migh'." His voice is low, only for me, his expression grave. "You migh' need it more than you realize, righ' now. My gut never fails me. And my gut tells me you're a good person." Anxiety tightens his mouth. Louder, he adds, "Now get ou' of here. And good luck, sirène."

I throw my arms around him, and he squeezes the air out of my lungs.

"Sirène?" Drew asks.

George and I answer in unison, "French for mermaid."

I start the engine while George mounts the jetty to release *Sassy* from her mooring. He and Drew exchange goodbyes and promises to visit. George sits on the jetty, dangles his sandaled feet over the side, and waves his pipe so vigorously, it's as if we're embarking on the America's Cup.

"I'll miss him," I tell Drew.

Drew's fingers thread through mine. "I can see that."

Once we're out of the bay, I switch off the motor and set up the windvane, aiming for Namua Island near Drew's resort. Drew sits at the bow, out of the way. When I'm done, I go to sit with him. He makes space for me between his legs, then rests his chin on my shoulder, arms around my waist. I savor every feeling, knowing I'll feed on them when we're apart. *I should stop doing this.* But if I back away now, he'll ask questions I can't answer. As far as he's concerned, he'll meet me in Australia. As far as he's concerned, we have a future. And I don't want to argue with him again.

I'll be gone by this time tomorrow.

The sky becomes blood red, sloshed with clouds dyed hot pink and plum.

Eventually, Drew presents the lobster, warm and dripping in garlic butter. We huddle, facing each other in the cockpit, inhaling it as if we haven't eaten in a week.

I point at the windvane. "George is the real deal. It's working."

"You should take him with you to Australia."

He said it . . . Australia.

Drew clears his throat. "He could be the captain."

"Not on *my* boat."

We laugh and Drew kisses my forehead, a simple touch that takes my breath away. We dunk our hands in a bucket of water to clean them.

"Did you visit Brett?" I ask.

Sorrow sprawls across Drew's face. "He didn't show. I waited for two hours. His flatmate got home and said he's not seen Brett in days. Said he's gone off the rails and stays out all night." Drew lifts his chin to me, unable to hide his unease.

I get up and burrow next to him. I can feel the weight of his torment as we stare out to sea and watch a rising orange moon that seems so close, we could paddle over and collect it in the dinghy.

"The resort's throwing a beach party tonight with Samoan dancers, a band, and a bonfire. Would you go with me?" Drew asks.

Except, it's better to stay hidden on *Sassy*. I shrug, avoiding his eyes.

When we reach Namua Island, I test the motor again, and Drew clears away the lobster. We circumnavigate the island, then lay anchor in Drew's Bay, my nickname for it.

It's our last night together, and I don't want to discourage him when he settles next to me in the cockpit. He pulls my legs across his lap, then asks me about my family. While I talk, I quietly notice the memories of my father don't crush and pound me as they used to, and I let it slip that my mother recently moved to Australia, and it's her and my uncle and brother I'm meeting in Townsville, Queensland. I hadn't meant to, because by the look of Drew's hopeful face, he immediately takes that as a positive sign for our future relationship.

"They're more boat crazy than me," I add. "Uncle Brody plans to give up his law practice to build boats full-time, and Finn dropped out of college to work on boats with him a few years ago." I'm babbling and try to push back the anxiety that's been building in me all day. "I've been wondering something . . . Did you tell me about George just so I'd come to this side of the island?"

Drew beams and pulls me under his arm. Ribbons of heat swirl through me. "I'll let you keep wondering about that." His voice is ragged and low. The memory of his touch last night increases my ache to kiss him, which is stronger than the need to pull on the reins. *One more kiss before I leave.*

I look up into a gaze that plunges into mine. His thumb strokes my cheek, a rawness in his expression knocks me sideways. His face moves closer as *Sassy* rises and falls with the waves. When his lips find mine, I pull back a smidge, our noses touching.

"I'm sorry I have to leave," I say, grazing his lips with mine, my breaths short and sharp.

"I know." His throaty words tumble into the night. Our

140

faces are so close, I can see the dancing flecks of blue in his eyes as our warm breath mingles. As if my mouth has a will of its own, it tilts up to his, and his lips part mine. "I'll come meet you," he says into my open mouth.

I close my eyes. Push away all negative thoughts.

His mouth is hot, soft, craving; fingers thread through my hair, pull me closer, deepening the kiss. My body curls into him, wants to climb under his skin. He tugs me onto his lap so I'm straddling him. Our lips come apart for a moment, but smash into each other again when he crushes me against him. I coil my arms around his neck and let go of everything else.

The sound of a police siren gouges the night.

I jump to my feet. A speedboat races to the west of the bay. Drew says something about police, but I don't hear because I'm already in the cabin starting the motor. I pull up the anchor, then dash behind the helm to steer into the black hole of the open sea.

"Shae? What are you doing?" Drew shouts.

"I have to get out of here."

"Why do I have the feeling I'm about to hear something I don't want to hear?"

Silence spills over us.

"Shae, you're scaring me." Drew plants his hand over mine on the helm.

I flick it away. "I shouldn't have stayed. I was pushing my luck. Serves me right."

His expression congeals. "More lies?"

"*No!* Not lies. Secrets." I watch his lips, the ones that just kissed me.

"Is it customs?"

It's a believable excuse. "Yes. I don't have my papers and I shouldn't be here. I didn't intend to anchor here and then the windvane broke . . ."

"Jeez, is that all?" Drew runs his fingers through his hair.

"Half the island works illegally. Don't worry, it'll be okay. Stop the boat before we end up at the North Pole." He hugs me, but it must be like hugging a ship's mast.

The speedboat circles the lagoon. The siren has stopped. Out of nowhere, a voice blares across the waves: "Bonfire party at Coconut Palm Beach Resort." A couple more police sirens cut the night sky before the message is repeated.

"It's just some jokers with a megaphone," Drew says. The megaphone makes bleep, bleep sounds, followed by a squeal and another police-style siren. "I just realized—they did the same thing for last month's beach party. I'd been in Samoa about a day at the time."

The speedboat whisks past us. Three guys wave and Drew waves back.

Lightheaded from adrenaline, I work to steer *Sassy* toward the resort.

Drew drops onto the bench seat. Without looking at me, he says the words I know have been poking around in his mind all evening. "Are you really leaving tomorrow?"

"Yes. I need to pick up diesel and fresh food in the morning. Then I must set sail."

"How long will the trip take?" It's the first time he's asked specifics about this leg of the crossing, as if he's avoided the thought of it.

"Not long. About three weeks. The first leg was over eight weeks. Luckily, this time I can bring loads of fresh fruit and—"

"I'm afraid something's going to happen to you." His voice is thick and strangled like twisted dough.

I watch as the stuffing falls out of him. *This is what I've feared. What I hoped to avoid.* I want to push him back together.

Imagine how much worse it'll be when he finds out the whole truth.

Sadness drenches me.

"Hey, after what I've survived," I say, falsely cheerful, "I can get through anything."

His eyes are gray and bleak. "I knew it'd be soon, but . . . a few more days?"

"It's going to be hard whenever I leave." The words come out as a strangled whisper. I avoid repeating George's cyclone worries in case it sets off another argument.

Drew suddenly stands and yanks the despondency from his face. "You're right. You've got to do what you need to do. We can meet up in Australia. I'd be the same. I do understand. It's just . . ." he searches my face as if rearranging it, "I only just found you."

"I know." I place my hand on his shoulder, and he covers it with his own as we motor the next few hundred meters in silence.

He volunteers to turn off the engine and when he returns, he says, "Do one thing for me? Let's enjoy the last night we'll have together for a while. Come to the beach party."

So he can't see my expression crumpling, I bury my face against him and nod. When I was stranded in the doldrums, I thought it was penance for my crime. But being alone at sea for weeks wasn't my punishment—leaving Drew is.

CHAPTER 19

Drew dumps his T-shirt on the bench seat and swims to the resort for a shower. I wonder when he plans to fetch it. Maybe I can take it with me to Australia, the only piece of him I'll get to keep.

After showering in the head using bottled water—my father had packed enough for six months—the urge to wear something different than my usual shorts and tank top outfit has me rifling through my mother's stash of clothes. Not much fits, but there's a burnt orange, sleeveless T-shirt dress that's tight and clingy for my mother but sits softly against my body. Music wafts across the water, and the resort is swathed in fairy lights so it resembles a vast spaceship on the beach. I scoot into shore in the dinghy using some old paddles George found. People gather next to a huge bonfire. Occasional loud laughter punches through the low murmur of voices.

I home in on Drew, which isn't hard because he stands out in a crowd. He's wearing an unbuttoned white shirt; it flaps in the warm breeze like a sail, revealing his abs and chest. The light-khaki shorts hang loosely from his hips. He swigs a beer and talks to Sienna and another girl. Sienna laughs and slaps him playfully on the arm. I hate the idea of leaving him on the island with her. He shifts from one foot to the other and swaps the bottle he's holding to his other hand. An older couple walks past and raises their wine glasses to him. He lifts his beer to them before giving his attention back to Sienna. Taking an imperceptible step backward, he looks over her head, searching. I leave the edges of the crowd to go to him.

It doesn't take a moment before he spots me. His grin is instant. He mouths, "Hey," across the gap between us. *Whoa. Breathe.*

Sienna spins round to discover who he's smiling at. I walk closer, touch Drew's arm, and reach to kiss his lips. My heart stretches, wide awake again.

He offers to buy me a drink. "Great dress," he says, his glance playful as he heads toward the bar. The bar area is teaming with people, and they've turned on the TV screens. I ball my fists, tensing inside—Drew can't see me on the news tonight.

Sienna asks, "So are you two . . . together?"

I shrug and peer at the other girl.

"Sorry, this is Harriet," Sienna says. "Harriet, this is Emily. She slept in our room the other night. What happened, by the way? Drew never said."

"I . . . it was too late to get a taxi."

Sienna explains to Harriet that I'm living on a boat and am about to leave for Australia. She re-tells how we met at the clinic and the village, then ponders me again. "Brett was here yesterday, looking for Drew," she says. "He asked a load of questions about you. Reckon he's got the hots—"

Drew nudges me with a tray holding four mini wooden bowls. "Kava. More authentic than bubbles," he says. We thank him in unison, and everyone finds a place to sit. Others join us, and we relax in a lumpy group on the beach, the light of the fire playing on our faces.

Louder music filters into the air, and twelve indigenous men wearing white cloths around their waists tramp onto the sand and form three lines.

"The Samoan slap dancers," Drew explains as they begin to shout and hoot in Samoan. They perform what appears to be a less aggressive version of the Maori haka, slapping their legs, arms, and chests and chanting what resembles a war cry. We watch and whoop with the singers. After they leave, a local band strikes up, encouraging everyone to dance.

The songs are soft and lilting, and Drew pulls me to my feet. At first, he's playful and spins me around, spiraling me out, pulling me in, and whirling me out again. The next time he twirls me, he grips my hip to stop the spin halfway so I'm facing away from him. I feel his chest through the back of my thin dress. He sways with me, his cheek resting on my head.

I soak him up—his lime and man-smell, the heat of him, how he likes me so much. His mouth slides to just under my ear where he kisses me, sending sparks flying around my body as if he's lit a sparkler in there. He coils and uncoils me again before stopping me once more, facing him this time. I'm giddy, and my mouth aches from smiling. Even though I've never danced with a man like this before, it's the most natural thing in the world to reach up and place my arms around his neck.

Drew's face is inches away. It's so intense that I turn to watch the pathway the moon unfolds across the ocean, but he catches my chin between his index finger and thumb and lifts my mouth to his. Pausing for a thrilling moment, his lips graze mine before opening my mouth into a deep, unhurried kiss. I melt into him. When the kiss ends, he collars my gaze, and I let myself wallow there.

The melodies echo the lapping waves and the curling of the palm trees, and the husky male harmonies wash over us. We lose ourselves, dancing among colorful couples but locked in our own world. Drew's kisses are lingering and tender; my fingers creep under his shirt, and I crawl into his blue eyes without self-consciousness.

Is this what it feels like to fall in love?

When the band takes a break, we join Drew's group of friends around the fire, listening to conversations about trips to rockslides, waterfalls, and Robert Louis Stevenson's grave, author of *Treasure Island*. Drew stretches out on his side beside me, propped on an elbow. He twirls a lock of my hair. Sienna watches us quietly, and I feel bad for her.

"Any chance I can convince you to stay a little longer?" he asks.

I move to sit cross-legged, plunge my fingers into the cool sand. *Why is he asking me to do something he knows I won't?* The smell of smoking wood isn't mellow or romantic anymore. It sticks in my throat. I rummage for the bottle of water. He passes it over, scrutinizing me, even though he already knows my answer.

"My family will be worried if I don't get there soon." *That's true.* I don't want to lie again. "And cyclone season . . ."

Drew's face cramps. He sits, elbows perched on bent knees.

"This is something I need to finish."

Drew's stare bores into the fire. "Are you sure there are no more . . . secrets?"

"No more secrets." *I'm so sorry for lying.*

For a moment, his face is naked, eyes trounced with hurt.

I've clipped the happiness right out of him.

"Better give you my email address," he says, trying and failing to smile.

I contemplate the stars, questioning if meeting again is a dream that can ever come true.

The band eventually leaves, but the resort staff continue to party around the crackling and popping bonfire in chatty, small groups. Someone brings out a guitar. A bloke named Chris plays and sings *Call Me Maybe,* and a girl with tattoos plays something jazzy she wrote before passing the instrument to me. I decline and pass it to Drew. I am surprised when he places it in his lap and strums a few chords. He plucks a melodic intro, his neck bent low, and kicks off with a song he tells us is *As Long as You Love Me*. His voice is tender yet strong. He glances around the group as everyone sways in the wavering firelight, the rolling breakers a gentle backdrop.

Then he watches me as he sings about not caring where his girl is from, or what she's done in her life, so long as she loves him. His smile fills me with light, like there are moon rays fooling around inside me. The others in the group ebb to the edge of my consciousness. I rock myself and settle into his gaze, electricity passes in the space between us as if we're trapped in a plasma lightning ball. But when Drew launches into the chorus, he encourages everyone to join in. He beams at the circle of people as we sing, raucous. I love that he's so comfortable in his own skin, so self-assured.

After loud applause and shouts for more, Drew picks up the pace with Train's *Hey, Soul Sister*. Everyone approves and leaps to their feet, shouting the words. I get up too, and we're jumping, jiving, spinning, clapping, our shadows copying and colliding as we renounce our cares. Drew strums and sings, sidestepping out a rhythm as he circles the group with the guitar, his features filled with a look of pure abandonment.

This time tomorrow, I'll be alone again, sailing across the Pacific. *He'll* be alone. My vision turns crooked through my tears.

"More, more," everyone shouts when Drew stops and passes the guitar to Harriet. She pushes it back to him.

"I've taken up enough of the spotlight," he says and passes it to another guy before homing in on me, his arm finally around my waist again. I lean into him, collect a tender kiss, one that splits the seams of my heart. Everyone focuses on Lochy, who gives a quirky rendition of *When You're Smiling*.

Sitting in the circle of Drew's legs, reality smarts. *We'll never have this again.*

"Want some water?" Drew whispers against my cheek. "I need to go to the toilet anyway." I nod. He kisses the top of my head, leaving his lips there for a few beats before standing and wandering up the beach to the bar. My teeth clench against tears. *This is it. Our last night together.* I decide I'll make love with Drew tonight. We're already in so deep, it won't make much difference. I doubt I've ever been truly made love to. Wishing Lochy would switch to a more upbeat tune, I hug my knees and think about being naked in Drew's arms.

Sand flicks against my back, and I twist round and into Brett's smirking face. He squats behind me, raises his bottle of beer as if toasting something. "Hello, *Girl Most Wanted by the Cops.*"

CHAPTER 20

B rett eyeballs me as if I'm a slice of chocolate cake he wants but can't have. He leans in, matching me as I tilt away from him. "I uncovered your secret."

Feeling drains out of me into the sand like blood from a mortal wound. I almost grab hold of him to stop the hurtling, falling sensation. "What secret is that?" My voice jars.

Brett's usual over-grown smile detonates across his face. "You didn't invite me to your soirée."

"We haven't seen you in a while." I fight to keep my voice firm and steady.

He takes a noisy swig of beer. "Not gonna slug me again, are you?" His smirk is sarcastic, but with a hint of humor. And he's slurring his words.

"That depends on if you're going to be a slime ball again." I clutch my knees and give the beach bar a furtive search. It's too dark to make out Drew.

Brett settles himself beside me, not crowding me for once. He inspects my feet, a vague smile crossing his lips.

"Spent last night in the local jail," he announces, then sniffs loudly. "Gotta tell you, they treat humans like pigs in there."

"Why were you in jail? What did you do?"

He snort-laughs. "I didn't do anything. There was this freakin' loser in this bar. I got into a fight. And the other night—" He sends his glance across the black ocean behind me, then stares directly at me. "I'm sorry, okay? It's no excuse, but I was drunk and maybe I read your signals wrong."

"What signals?"

He puts up both hands as if at gunpoint. "Okay, okay. I said I was sorry."

I let handfuls of sand sift through my fingers. Brett leans in closer, and I grip the sand. "I'm warning you." I sit straighter and shake my sand-filled fists at him, only half-joking.

"Yeah, I got it. You're friggin' lethal." He rubs the lip I had bitten and continues to inspect me. Curious. Boyish. A smirk lifts the corner of his mouth. "I was watching you and Drew. You hooked up?"

My index finger makes circles in the sand and I struggle to calm my breathing.

Brett lets out a sound that's half-cough, half-spit. "So why him and not me? What's he got that I don't?"

"Don't ask questions you won't like the answers to."

"Yeah. You're right. He's a much better person than me." He smooths the lumps of sand he's made. His hand freezes mid-air. "It's why I gotta do what I gotta do."

"What are you talking about?"

"You were too mysterious. That was a big red flag. Your boat's name is hard to forget."

The end of my story, my journey, rushes up on me as unavoidable as rain.

"And when Sienna mentioned how Drew calls you Shae . . ."

I watch his moving lips as if they're not part of him but floating in space.

"I know your name is Shae Love. I know you're on the run. I know..."

My breath rises sharply, and there's a whooshing noise in my ears so I can't hear him, can only watch his lips shovel words at me.

"...a big reward for any information that leads to finding you. It's all there, on the internet." Brett chuckles, then sucks on his beer.

As if swimming upward and breaking the surface of the ocean, I come back to myself, pull air into my lungs. I push onto my knees, scan the beach for Drew. Knots of people dance around the fire, others slouch in groups drinking, even though it must be after midnight.

Brett moves closer, inches from me. "Always knew there was something different about you."

I swallow hard against the awareness of being trapped.

"I wanted to get to know the girl who solo sails the Pacific, the girl who can evade the cops for so long. The Gotta Go Girl who fights her own battles. I'm quite a good catch. Shame you didn't choose me. How about you give Drew the flick, and I'll keep my mouth shut? We can hide out together." His hand slumps onto my knee, punting me out of the swamp in my head and transforming bogginess to glittering anger.

I shuffle sideways and smack at his arm. "Why do you always compete with Drew? Can't you find your own girls? You can't blackmail someone into liking you."

Brett pops his neck, failing to hide the hurt that flits across his features. "That was a test. And you passed." He cracks his knuckles. "But there are a couple of things going on here. Number one is that Drew's my buddy, and we look out for each other. Have since kindergarten. We'll do anything for each other. Drew even took the rap for me once —spent the night in jail. Saved my useless hide. Now *that's* brotherhood."

"Sounds one-sided to me."

"You're not wrong there. I'm always stuffing up. Now it's my turn to do something for Drew. I have to tell him what I know about you."

"No!"

A clown-sized smile creeps onto his lips. "Quite a reaction. So, he *doesn't* know. What's the game plan?"

The smoky air clogs my throat. "I'm not playing any games."

"You're not another gold digger after his inheritance?"

"What inheritance?"

"Is Drew the next victim after Connor Stratton? Ready to kill again for all that money?"

I gulp at the sound of Connor's name. "Money isn't a reason to kill."

Brett chuckles. "What if it's billions? Not heard of the Vega family?"

"No. Should I?"

"You're a good actress. Of course, you know of them. And Drew's always struggled to find someone who didn't love him for his money. You're just like Ava. That's why she's his ex. Except, it appears you'd even kill for it."

"Get lost, Brett." I stare him down, but his expression turns cruel.

"It's *you* who needs to leave. I won't let you play your games with Drew any longer. I'm stepping in."

"I promise you. He doesn't need protecting from me."

"He doesn't even know your real name."

Rising to my feet, I grasp the sand and throw it at Brett. He spits and jumps up. His height and sour smell as he exhales into my face reminds me of the night he attacked me. But he doesn't touch me this time. Instead, he paces in circles. Someone plucks the guitar, and a few people, including Sienna, give us sidelong glances.

Brett stops, hands on hips, towering over me. "You'll find

Drew values honesty. I lied to him once about my new talent for thieving stuff. He was more bothered about the lying than the thieving. Put our friendship right on the line."

Panic lunges into my chest. I start my own pattern of pacing, moving away from the group.

"Are you even listening to me?" Brett shouts.

I stop in front of him, stare into callous eyes. "Brett. Please don't. I'm leaving tomorrow anyway. I'll turn myself in soon. I just have to get somewhere first."

A smile ghosts across his face. "And like I said, there are a *couple* of things going on here. And the second thing is . . ." he looks down the beach, brings his shoulder and the side of his head together as if he has an itchy ear, "I need the reward."

"Drew said your family's loaded and they send you whatever money you need."

"And he's not wrong. But I can't rely on them forever. You've no idea what they have put me through. I'm never going home again. Except after I got arrested yesterday, I had to call my dad and ask him to cover the damages the bar is suing me for. Just like before, he's threatening to disinherit me. He'd rather all the cash went to my half-sisters anyway, so he was just looking for an excuse. The money's going to stop soon."

He holds up a hand, and I step back at the sight of his missing pinkie finger. He must have lost it a long time ago because it's a neat nub of flesh. "I've run out of prosthetics, too. They're not exactly cheap."

"Your father cut your finger off?"

"No. But he may as well have." Brett shrugs, a great galumphing wounded bear, slightly apologetic. "The police are going to catch you anyway. I might as well have a million bucks in my back pocket before they do. Then I can set myself up and never see my bastard father again."

I clutch his arm. "Please don't."

He stares at my fingers. "My mind's made up. There's nothing you can say to change it."

This is it, the moment I've been afraid of.

Right here, right now.

"I have to tell Drew tonight," Brett adds. "I like you. You don't seem like the violent type but for all I know, his life is in danger."

A whimper slews from my mouth. "Have you told the police?"

He scrunches his shoulders, shoves his hands into his pockets. "Not yet. I wanted to talk to Drew first." Brett points behind me. "He's coming."

Drew's white shirt flaps in the night breeze as he ambles down the steps from the bar. He's carrying two bottles of water. Something inside me crumples.

I let him believe we have a future.

Only hours ago, I promised him there were no more secrets. *There's too much for him to forgive. Too many lies. Like Brett, he'll think I had him in my sights as my second victim.*

I take a step backward from Brett, my chin juddering. He lunges at me, but he's too drunk and slow. I twist away and run.

"Tell Drew I said goodbye. And that I'm sorry." My voice is thick and cuts out as if my throat is filled with wet sand. I doubt Brett even heard me.

CHAPTER 21

Strains of a guitar ballad from the party follow me on the breeze. I dare to check over my shoulder, nearly tripping over my own feet. Behind me, Drew is watching me and raises his arm, but I can't hear his words. He breaks into a run. Through my tears, the blurred beach resembles a crumpled, ripped image of itself.

I keep running. The light's so dim at the southern end that I dash past the dinghy. Drew will catch up before I can push it into the water anyway. I run noiselessly into the dark ocean. It swallows me in one gulp.

Underneath the waves, it's pure black, and I'm sobbing so hard I'm forced to surface. I thump through the ocean. I'm tearing in two, half of me reaching for Drew on the beach, the other half being yanked toward *Sassy* as if she's my anchor, and she's hauling me in.

I don't have a choice.

But it all changes again. Drew is there, grabbing my feet, my legs, my waist. He wears the hurt on his face, a torn mask. A breaker lifts us. "What are you doing?" he shouts.

"I . . . I have to go. It's too hard to say goodbye."

"Come back to shore. This is awful. You can't leave like

this. I don't even know how to contact you." His eyes are wild.

A wave dumps on us, forcing us under. We resurface in waist-high water. Drew links his fingers through mine. "Brett said you'd gone and to say goodbye. Why are you running away from me?" The waves shove and prod us. Drew takes my other hand. Our gazes link. "What aren't you telling me?" His face is battered with confusion.

I can't lie anymore.

I look at him, into him, willing him to understand, and to let me go without needing to know more.

"Shae? Please." A ridge as thick as a pencil carves into his brow.

My chest glitches.

A shadowy figure lurches toward us. "You know her real name is Shae Love?" We swing round to face Brett, who's knee deep in the surf, holding Drew's white shirt. "She's on the run from the law, Drew. I'm guessing you didn't know that. She's wanted—"

A wave crashes over our shoulders and Brett's next words are drowned out. He's still talking when I emerge and wipe the salty water from my face.

"There's even a reward. A cool million bucks." His words crackle around us like debris from an explosion.

Drew's expression slips and slides, then smarts and stiffens, unraveling the clues. *Working out it's the truth.* He lets my fingers slip away.

"She's a fugitive. A criminal. You can't trust her . . . not in your position. She's just another gold digger," Brett shouts louder than ever. I want to chuck a tidal wave at him.

Comprehension inches across Drew's face. And there it is —the look I've been so afraid of. His eyes pool with the mayhem of truth. I twist back to *Sassy*, sure he'll let me go now. And for a few steps, he does. But then he clasps my wrist. "Stop running from me."

157

I stare at *Sassy*. My ribcage tightens. It doesn't take much to yank myself free of his grip. I lunge through the swell. Drew follows me deeper into the waves and grabs my hand again.

"You have to tell me the truth, Shae. *Once and for all.*" The cords of his voice are sweet and tender, softly wrapping his lips around my name.

I stare over his shoulder at Brett, who's shouting something we can't hear over the surf. "I argued with my boyfriend. I-I ran away." *That's not a lie.* "And I'm here illegally. Customs. I must get out of here. Brett's going to call the police and report me." *That's true, too.*

Drew releases my hand. "Why are you lying to me?" he says through gritted teeth, but his face is fragile like it might splinter at any moment.

I spin round and wade deeper just as a breaker rams me backward. When I stand, we're barely a meter apart. In the distance, still on the beach, Brett waves his arms at us, but we're too far away to hear what he's shouting.

"I'm not lying." My lie drops between us, cracks open.

He crushes his lips into a straight line. "You're. Still. Lying." The chaos and distress that spool off him is almost visible, like waves of rippling heat.

I can't say the words. I can't bear to see his reaction to the truth.

It's better he hears my story from Brett when I'm gone.

"If customs catch me—"

Drew gestures to halt my words. His stare gouges me. I witness the betrayal and the resentment and the disappointment that's cutting through his core—it comes crashing out of his eyes, rolling and tumbling, and lands at my feet.

But the truth is too big.

His expression becomes stony and critical; they cut past my defenses, peeling away the lies, seeking the nub of truth.

"Go then! I won't stop you!" His mouth twists, his chin

quivering. "Every time I think we're becoming close, you become more of a stranger. I guess I'll find out the truth one day, but it won't be from your lips." When he veers away from me, it's as if he's planted a bomb inside my heart. It detonates and hollows me out.

I turn to *Sassy*, pieces of me flying in every direction.

CHAPTER 22

Under spiky stars, *Sassy* motors away from the lagoon and into the open sea. My hurt is so deep, the tears can't get out.

There's a strong wind, and I make myself move to set up the sails—sail power will be swifter than the motor, not to mention quieter. Drew sits in the center of my mind and I do everything wrong such as setting the sails before turning off the engine. I grab the helm just in time to avoid a gibe. It takes ten minutes to do what should take a few moments but eventually, *Sassy* urges faster through the water, guided by the windvane. At one point, I imagine Drew's voice calling me, but the beach is a spark of light in the far distance.

I've left the dinghy on the beach. It's proof for Brett and the police.

Inside the cabin, the ghost of Drew lives like a caress in the air. After changing into dry clothes, I crash onto the bunk and hug the gray T-shirt he left behind. I inhale the coconut and lime scent of him. Everything is in pieces, a smashed jigsaw puzzle of a life with the center of the puzzle missing. My arm drops out of the bunk as if reaching for the hand of Drew's ghost. My eyelashes rest in pools of tears. After an hour of not caring if we hit a tanker, I set an alarm. When it beeps thirty minutes later, I'm caked in misery and can barely get up.

I go through the usual checks, chiding myself to get *Sassy* moving faster—after all, Brett could've already called the police. But the sight that clouts me as I inspect the horizon makes my pulse riot.

The Jesus line is pulling someone along. His head hangs down and to the side so I can't see his face, and his arms stretch overhead to grip the towrope. I'd know that head and those arms anywhere. I call to him.

He doesn't move. At least ninety minutes have passed since I set off. How's he hung on for so long?

He might even be dead.

I work to slow *Sassy*, heave to; the swells are large but gentle, so they don't break. As *Sassy* decelerates, Drew's head moves. I lean over the gunwale, pull the rope hand over fist, dragging him closer. He's tied the end of the rope into a loop under his arms, like a noose, so he didn't need to hang on the whole time. That action saved his life.

The best access onto *Sassy* is at the back of the boat where there's a sloped ledge rather than a steep side. Drew bobs in the water, but he's too weak to do anything more than cling to the lower bar of the lifelines, his head hanging. If only I could see his face. I loop the rope to make a foothold.

"Find the rope foothold, Drew. You can step up." After a pause, he takes in a deep breath, steps into the loop, and pulls up to a standing stance behind the boat. "You're a freaking maniac," I add.

He blinks, then gives me a wry smile that cleans out my heart. "I forgot my T-shirt."

"You're a funny guy." I laugh, ridiculously relieved that he's telling jokes.

He slips into the cockpit in the grip of a coughing fit. He's wearing the khaki shorts, but no shirt, and the rope has chafed and cut the skin under his arms and across his back. He winces as I untie and pull it away, and the wounds pool with blood now that he's out of the sea.

"I'll fetch you some water," I say, "but I have to get *Sassy* moving again. Then we'll sort you out, okay?" He rests his arms on the bench seat and slumps against it.

I re-set the sails and we're waltzing across the ocean again. When I return to the cockpit, Drew's fast asleep in the well. With nothing to do but cover him with a sheet, I scrutinize him from the cabin roof, afraid to consider what could've happened. I hadn't imagined him calling my name, either—he was behind the boat the whole time.

He came after me. The breath curdles in my throat.

He'll want the truth.

While Drew sleeps, I change out of the orange dress and rummage through the aft storage for my father's clothes. Drew has nothing to wear except the wet shorts he's wearing and the gray T-shirt he left behind yesterday. As I open the bag, my nose prickles with my father's leather and clove scent. I shove my face into the clothes, letting my tears soak them. I fall asleep, my cheek resting on his shirts, and when I wake, daylight floods the cabin. I'd forgotten to re-set the AIS and rush to check the horizon.

Drew's sitting in the well of the cockpit, leaning against the bench seat. His arms rest on bended knees. He stares into space, expressionless. The sight of his vacant features scares me.

"You're awake," I say, attempting to sound cheery.

His shoulders rise as if he's remembered to breathe. He looks hollowed out.

"Can I fetch you something to eat, Drew?"

He frowns at some invisible point, so detached from me, he may as well be back on the beach. All the confusion and betrayal I saw last night gang up in his face again.

I place a bottle of sunscreen next to him. "At least let's

sort you out. You're bleeding. And you should come out of the sun."

When he looks up, his eyes seem to bark at me. "The reason you ran away . . ." he says. "It's not simply because of an argument with your ex-boyfriend or you'd have told me." His voice is calm, but flint-like. He stares unhappily out to sea.

Tears pricking, I glare back, refusing to lie even one more time, yet unable to spill the truth—wouldn't it make everything worse? Drew risked his life for nothing—for a liar and for someone he can't be with. Accident or not, Connor is dead.

When I don't respond, Drew grips his knees. His mouth contorts. I search for the look that makes me feel as if he's drinking me in, possibly falling for me, but it's gone.

"I just risked my life on that towrope," Drew grits out. "What more do I need to do to earn your trust?" He climbs onto the roof and chucks his empty water bottle into the cockpit. But it's not about trust anymore.

Scuttling into the cabin, I double over, strap my hand across my mouth to lock away the sobs. I suck in slices of air through my fingers. I'm revolted at myself for the lies, for hurting him, but worse, with all that anger grinding through him, I'm afraid. How well do I know him after so few days? He could turn on me like my dad and Connor and Brett. We're alone on this boat . . . I glance at the locker that contains the gun.

After setting the AIS alarm, I lay low in the bunk, torn between going to the Drew I think I know and fetching the gun to protect myself from the Drew he might be.

An hour later, the rhythm and sound of the ocean against *Sassy* changes; the wind gauge reads a strong nineteen knots. I head up top to trim the sails. The sight of Drew makes my soul clench. His cheerless face tilts to the sky as the tumbling rain washes away the blood from his torso.

163

"You're going to fall overboard if you stay up here in these squalls," I say, intending to go below myself. He ignores me as I work on the winch. "Drew, you need to get in the cockpit."

He doesn't move.

I dive below to prepare some food, but instead, I'm crashing pots and tins, on the verge of throwing them. *Sassy* lurches, making me bang my hip. Rubbing the bump, I grab a handhold but stagger backward in fright.

Drew is right there.

He folds his arms, his expression gritty and stern. A sliver of fear slides through me. I stare back, clutching the galley sink behind me. An image of Connor wearing a similar expression blazes. *Men are Jekyll and Hydes.* Brett can be charming and entertaining, but he has an intimidating side to him, a part of him that could turn on you. Maybe Drew does too, it's just buried deeper.

"Are you going to tell me the truth?" Drew's words are whips snapping the air.

My breath stutters. My eyes dart for somewhere comfortable to rest. They settle for a porthole. "There's nothing to tell." My voice is thin, fading sea mist.

"You're terrified of the police to the point you'd leave without saying goodbye and you'd risk your life by setting off with cyclone season around the corner, *simply because you had a row with your boyfriend?* Why couldn't you just stay in Samoa?" His voice gets louder. My face warps. "And your uncle is a lawyer and what a coincidence . . . he lives in the very place you absolutely must reach without delay. Why is there a million-dollar bounty on your head? Why do you need a lawyer?"

My chin shudders. Tears swarm. I clamp my lips tight and stare him down.

"I *need* to know. Whatever's happened, I'm part of it now. I'm an accomplice. Tell me the truth, Shae."

When he says my name, it plucks at my heartstrings, but I turn my back on him. "Why didn't you just go back to the beach and ask Brett?"

He slams a Coleman lantern through the companionway opening, smashing it across the cockpit. "Dammit, Shae! I need to hear this from *you*. Do you think I trust Brett?"

I crush the fear that storms into me and try to push past him to escape onto the deck. He grabs my wrists and walks me backward. The physical power he has over me . . .

I hate it. He could kill me with his bare hands. I glance at the locker containing my father's gun. Images of my mother drill into my brain—the fights, the punches, the arguments. I'd only ever snuck out to witness a fight once, but once was enough. I slid along the wall of the hallway, peered through my parents' half-opened bedroom door. The tips of my father's shoes poked out from behind the door, the black-patent ones, shiny and a bit pointed. His breathing sounded as if he'd been running hard. My mother was hunkered in a ball on the carpet, arms tightly wrapped around her legs, head rammed between her knees. The scene is forever burned into my retinas like a tattoo. Then there was Connor. Behind his good looks, his brains, his money, he was a monster, too. Then Brett. Therefore, Drew's capable of over-powering me.

I wrench my wrists free and pummel at him, kicking out. "Don't you *ever* . . . How *dare* you? Don't you *ever* hit me." It's like I'm erupting. I want to hurl fireballs into the sky. And at Drew.

Drew steps back. "I wasn't going to hit you," he shouts. "I grabbed your wrists because I'm frustrated that you keep running from me."

"Don't you get it? I *can't* tell you. The truth is too big. It's too awful. And you'll hate me for the lies because I let you get close knowing what I know. Knowing we can't be together.

Everything we shared, everything we were, will be broken and changed."

"I could never hate you. Don't you know that?" He's still shouting. "And I could never hit you."

I stand my ground as we glower at each other.

Drew swallows and lowers his voice. "When you left me in the waves, I went half-crazy trying to understand. One thing I did know is whatever your reason for running away, I had to be there with you to help you through it." He takes my face in his hands. The fury bubbling inside me reduces to a simmer. "And I was sure if you'd done something bad, it couldn't be *that* bad because I know—*I know* you couldn't do anything really terrible. I went through what it could be and realized even if you'd robbed a bank or . . . or killed someone—"

A sob, stuck in my chest moments before, catapults into the small space between us.

Drew's mouth pulls downward. His eyes bloat and shimmer with tears. He relinquishes my face and takes a step away.

"Whatever you did, it wasn't on purpose," he adds. "That's what I thought. You didn't plan it. I knew it—would've been . . . an accident, a mix up." His words clunk out, each sentence attached to an anxious, unraveling thought leading toward that lightbulb moment. My lips distort. I let out another sob. "And so, I needed to be with you . . . and that's when I . . . I dove into the ocean and came after you."

I can't stop shuddering and swallowing tears and watching him crack open my secret.

He squeezes his eyes tight as if to block out the truth. His body droops, his fingers drag through his hair and clutch at his scalp.

After a few minutes, he lifts his face, inspects me from under heavy eyelids. "You killed someone?"

My crying turns wild and I stumble backward. Drew

moves with me, cloaks me with his arms. He's shaking, too. One of his hands holds my head tight against his shuddering chest, and we cling to each other as if we're plunging together into a bottomless abyss. If I could stop crying, I'm certain I'd hear Drew's sobs.

Eventually, we become silent, and Drew's trembling stops. He loosens his hold on me. "What happened?" He speaks into my hair. The heat of his breath comforts. His voice sounds tender, caressing.

I cling to him. *It's time.*

I gulp down another sob. "My dad—"

It's as if there's a stick of liquorice in my throat, blocking and choking me. I mash my face into Drew, fight the despair, then straighten.

"My dad beat my mom. All the time." The words out, I step back and collapse onto the wet seat behind me. "It's complicated. But I-I never did anything to stop him. We have defective genes. I'm like her. I let my boyfriend, Connor, hit me, too. I didn't stop him. I didn't know how to leave him. He was all I had. I am weak. My father died. Mom moved to Australia. Connor's moods got worse. He got into a rage if I spent too much time sailing or out of the house. He forced me to choose between sailing and college. He wouldn't let me work. Sometimes he followed me when I went out. He accused me of sleeping with every sailing student I met at the club, even though Connor was my first and only. We fought about it. Always ending in him punishing me. If he thought I'd taken an extra shift teaching sailing, we'd fight. He locked me in the laundry room to punish me. Naked, so I couldn't climb out the window. He was working on making me give up sailing, too. I was trapped. I had no money of my own. No friends. He had made sure of that. I was afraid of him. Yet, I thought I loved him."

I let the words fall from my mouth, let them scatter into the cabin as if dropping a heavy burden of rocks. "And . . .

and then he really hurt me. I can't describe it. He was a monster and I was his rag doll. I thought I was going to die. I tried to warn him off with a knife, but he was so strong. He turned the blade on me. I didn't mean to. I didn't. But somehow. I stabbed him. I killed him."

Drew doesn't move or say a word.

CHAPTER 23

I sit on the wet seat and wait for my words to sink in, breath clutched in my ribcage. Minutes soak up more minutes. Drew reaches out, caresses my hair behind my ears. I breathe again.

"We'll get through this." His whisper is bony, bewildered —it doesn't match his words. He pulls me to my feet and cups my elbows. "Is that why you thought I was going to hit you?"

"I won't let *anyone* treat me like that again."

"Let's get this straight right now. I would *never, could never,* hurt you like that."

"How do you know? You can't say *never*."

He straightens and rubs the back of his neck with this hand. "Jeez, Shae. That's just something you know about yourself."

I recall my father's letters and how he knew there was a monster inside him. He worked to hide it, to kill it. But doesn't every man have a tipping point, that moment of no return when they're pushed too far and use their physical strength to strike? Even Drew got angry—he threw that lantern. What would've happened if I'd pushed him a bit further?

"You don't *know*, Drew. You can't." I step forward and shove him. "You assume it's not in you, but it's there." I thrust at him again, and his arms fling sideways to steady himself. His face reveals no anger, just an uprising of confusion. "All men have it. You know you have that ultimate power over women. You hang out with Brett. He tried to force himself on me. And you're still friends. I mean, there's nothing right about that." With his back against the nav table and with no place to shove him, I clench a fist to punch him—to push him to his tipping point. To show him I'm right. "Maybe you *don't* disapprove of Brett's behavior."

Drew grabs my fist before it makes contact. "Not all men," he shouts. "Your father, yes. Connor. Even Brett. But I believe your dad was born with DNA that meant he was the sort of man who lost his temper quickly and couldn't hold it back." His hand still covers my fist. "But that's not in me." His expression begs, aching to reach me.

I wrench away. "You could change. Connor and Brett did. Everyone does, and not usually for the better. You could become someone who—"

"I bet you weren't the first girl Connor hurt. Do you think *you* could suddenly become someone who, I don't know, kicks dogs? You'd know if you had it in you, and I—most guys—don't have it in us to batter our girlfriends."

I would never hurt a dog or anything weaker than me. Like Drew said, I just know that.

Drew reaches to push my hair behind my ears, but I jerk back and whack away his arm.

"You can't deny you lost your temper," I shout. "You threw that lantern. You were so close to losing control."

"But I wouldn't have hit *you*." He folds his arms. "Have you never lost your temper and chucked something? I'd have thrown everything I could get hold of, punched a wall,

170

kicked a hole in the hull before I hit you. The difference between me and Connor is that I know when to stop, where the line you don't cross is. Didn't I pull back the moment you yelled at me?"

I couldn't disagree. He had folded away his anger from something huge and uncontrolled, like stuffing a parachute into a small box. He also hated himself for hitting Brett that night on the beach. I reflect on how I just goaded Drew to lose his temper and hit me. Deep down, I know I only did that because I knew he wouldn't.

Turning my back to him, I hug myself. "Do you think I might have my mom's DNA?"

"I've known you for only a few days and even I know the answer to that. Do you really believe you resemble your mother? Be honest with yourself."

I had confronted Connor when my mother had never confronted my father, even after my dad broke her arm. And I braved the Pacific alone, despite being 'just a girl.' I fought back against Brett. If anything, I've become *less* like my mother.

Behind me, Drew moves closer but doesn't touch me. "Reckon any bloke tried anything, you'd rip their head off. Thought I was a goner earlier."

Something inside me slips and loosens. "I'm not my mom now. But what if I *become* her? She changed." The fight has gone from my voice, though. I drop my face into my hands. My body sags.

Drew places his hands on my shoulders and squeezes. "You don't automatically grow up to be your parents, you know. You can choose *not* to be like your mom. You already have."

"As you did . . . I mean, choosing not to be like your dad?"

"I never thought of it in that way. But I suppose so."

Neither of us move. The warmth of Drew's hands on my shoulders soak through me, a healing balm. It's only then that the noise of flogging sails reach me. Despite feeling as if a tsunami recently swept through me, I need to go on deck.

"I have to see to *Sassy*, or we could jibe, worst case, lose the mast."

"Sailor first, woman second," he says, but his voice is limp.

While I work the winches, Drew settles on the cabin roof. I want to talk more and so I head below to flick on the engine. It doesn't turn over the first time. Or the second. *I was supposed to buy more diesel.* It's not the worst problem. I made it to Samoa without a motor because my father hadn't loaded the diesel yet.

Instead, I re-set the sails, every now and then stealing glances at Drew. He leans against the mast, his eyes two voids, arms hugging his knees.

He looks like someone unplugged him.

He's regretting his choice to come after me. Does he see me in a different light?

The truth is too big, too much to accept—no matter what he says.

At the nav station, I work out if it's possible to set Drew down on a nearby island. The tension stretched and fraying, I droop over the table and grit my teeth against tears. Drew is suddenly there and tugging me to him. The breath whooshes out of my lungs.

"I will never hurt you." His words are close, hot on my face; they wrap around me like a life jacket. "It's going to be okay. But we need to talk this through. Come." He guides me to the cockpit where the sky has whipped up a mango smoothie sunset.

"Connor? You were at home when it happened?" he asks.

Sitting next to him on the bench seat, I nod. "He had attacked me . . . hurt me badly. He was getting more smashed, and he was coming for me again. I grabbed the knife to warn him off."

I recall how Connor was stronger than me, even when he

was drunk. He had wrestled the knife from my grip and punched me until I couldn't hold up my head—it lolled, chin on my chest. The edges of my vision blurred, and I believed that was it. He was going to kill me.

Connor had let me sag to the ground, then pinned me with his body and put the blade to my cheek. "Soon, I'm going to use this to cut off that tattoo I told you not to get." He spat in my face and threw the knife aside. His eyes stabbed at me and I knew he wasn't joking.

I stare at the sea eagle on my ankle as I tell Drew what happened. Drew helmets his head, trembling. I've never seen a man truly cry, and it's a shock to recognize men can be vulnerable, too.

Finally, I open my mouth to force out the final part. "It was the fact he was drunk that saved me. He seemed to forget about the knife." He had kissed me roughly, kneading and shoving at my body, and I maneuvered us closer to where he'd thrown it.

Drew's eyes well up again. "I can't bear to think about what you went through."

He's crying for me.

"He was a monster and deserved to die." Drew's words skid between gritted teeth. He jumps up and spins a full circle, kicks at the bench seat before dropping into a squat, one hand on each of my knees. He hunts inside my face for something.

I tumble into his eyes. "I'm sorry for lying to you."

"It's no wonder you couldn't trust anyone."

"That's why I pushed you away and said I didn't want a holiday romance. I'm going to go to prison for the rest of my life."

"You don't deserve that. It was self-defense."

"They'll call it excessive force." My voice cracks. "I didn't need to kill him, did I?"

Drew caresses my cheek with the backs of his fingers. "I

don't know how the law will see it. All I know is you saved yourself." He sits beside me and slips an arm around my shoulders. "Life imprisonment isn't in the cards though. Maybe you'll do some time, but not life. They must understand it as self-defense. What if he'd killed you?"

"But I need to prove that. He came from the respected Stratton family. He was a stockbroker, a part of the elite set. No one knew he hit me. They all thought we were happily in love. And as far as everyone's concerned, he was an upstanding member of the community. He even donated to charities. They'll think I did it for his inheritance. Even Brett thought that."

"We'll fight it. It's not a foregone conclusion. What else were you meant to do? You were in fear of your life. Your uncle's a lawyer, right?"

Drew's words waft inside me, breaths of fresh air, and for the first time since that night, I accept that I don't deserve to be punished. I let his words float in my mind, turning them over until I not only comprehend them, but allow myself to believe them.

The grip guilt has on me loosens a little.

"Do you think Brett will go to the police to collect the reward?" I ask.

Drew cracks his knuckles and sits beside me again. "I don't know . . . If you'd asked me three months ago, I'd have said no. I'm not sure now."

"What did Brett mean about you not being able to trust me *in your position?*"

We sit facing each other on the same bench seat, our knees drawn up. Drew digs his toes underneath mine and pushes our bare feet together as if we're doing a high-five. He smirks, wistful. "My father . . . He's well known in Australia. An influential businessman, shall we say. And very wealthy. The media plagues him and would have a party if his son got into trouble—or was hanging out with a girl wanted for . . . for murder."

"I'm not a gold digger."

"That's the only thing I am sure about right now."

"Why does Brett have a missing finger?"

"He told you?"

"He showed me. He said he needed another prosthetic and that his father was going to disinherit him, and that's why he must turn me in and claim the reward."

"Shit." Drew moves his feet off the bench seat and onto the deck, disconnecting our contact. "That's not good."

"You think he'll inform the police?"

"Let's just say, his father disinherited him once before. He doesn't like me talking about it, but that's how he lost the finger." Drew squints at a flickering light on the darkening horizon.

"I need to check the radar . . . that's a ship." I leap down the three stairs into the cabin, then come up top to tack until we're no longer on a collision course. The ship turns out to be a cruise-liner. It looms closer, the size of a tower block. Its lights twinkle, a giant, ghostly Christmas tree as it glides past us, eight hundred meters to our stern.

"Skillfully done, captain," Drew says from the companionway hatch. He'd been crashing around in the cabin for a while. "Reckon I'll be more useful in the kitchen though. I'm starving. Ready for something to eat?"

The thought of food makes me nauseous, but I say, "Sure. It's called a galley though. Not a kitchen."

Drew disappears below again, and my mind returns to Brett. It's impossible to know if he'll go to the police but Brett didn't seem like the kind of man to turn his back on a million dollars or put a friendship first.

CHAPTER 24

Later that night, *Sassy* heels so hard a large part of her hull is out of the water. The wind slaps her. Forked lightning stabs the sea in the distance.

"Drew. Drew! You need to go below."

Drew is at the bow, hanging on the lifelines on the port side. His grin is thrilled. He can't hear me.

"You're not wearing a harness."

We'd fallen asleep in the well of the cockpit, and now it's pitch dark with a wild and whistling wind. While I was checking the charts below and turning on the lights, Drew went exploring on deck.

My chest splinters with fear. "Come back, Drew." But the gale snatches my words away. I clip into a harness and move rapidly toward him. Salty spray stings my face. He finally sees me beckoning and palms his way into the cockpit. A breaking wave jumps up to the port side and drenches us. Drew simply laughs.

"Please go below." I shout to compete with the wind's whine.

"No, I can help."

"You haven't got a harness." I pull at my own. "Another time. Don't make it more difficult for me."

He nods through the powdery spray and disappears into the cabin, shutting the hatch behind him. Now I must save us both.

I struggle with the angle we're sailing on and put a third reef in the mainsail. The sail spills some air, and *Sassy* rights herself. The air currents keep shifting, forcing me to adjust and readjust the sails, but the sheeting rain and zippy wind make it harder and harder. Drew's face emerges in a porthole, etched with worry. The storm jib checked, I throw out the anchor and head below.

"Wicked wind," I say as I charge through the hatch.

Drew's changed into my father's clothes and leans against the bunk wearing too-loose shorts and a light gray tracksuit top. The hood is pulled up over his wet hair, but he hasn't zipped up, as if he's on some catalogue modeling shoot with his six-pack on display. I tug my stare away and study the instruments. It's midnight. And I don't like what's on the radar.

"Is it a cyclone?" Drew asks.

"No." *Not yet.* "Remember I told you about knockdowns?"

"I was afraid you were going to say that."

"We'll be okay. *Sassy's* a strong boat." I point at his shorts which are too loose around his hips. "I'll cut some rope."

After making his belt, I fetch dry clothes and change in the privacy of the head. When I come out, Drew's clutching the roof handholds. He flashes a flirtatious smile that reaches his eyes. "Shy, are you?"

I turn away to hide the flush that swells my cheeks.

"You need to teach me to sail so I can be useful to you," he adds. "I feel like a complete dill watching you do everything."

"But maybe not tonight?" To prove my point, the wind shrieks and clobbers *Sassy*. We lurch, and it's as if every person who ever died at sea gathers to screech at us. I show

Drew how to hold on and what stance to take. The back of the boat bucks, and *Sassy* surfs another swell. We reach the trough and straighten before *Sassy* lunges up the next one.

I hear the roar of a wave approaching, as loud as an express train. I yell, *"Brace."*

We're slapped over, and the portholes go green on the starboard side. It's a small knockdown, not even ninety degrees, and *Sassy* zips up. Drew is still grinning.

"Better than a bungee jump?" I ask.

"Way scarier. Can't believe you did this all by yourself."

"I'm just a girl, after all."

"That's rubbish. You can do anything you put your mind to. I've been watching you. You're amazing."

It's one of the reasons I like Drew so much—he makes me feel like I have no limits.

Lightning juts ethereal shapes across our features and thunder rumbles overhead, the storm keeping us fixed to our stations for an hour. When it blows itself out, I go on deck for a damage check. Luckily, this storm spared us.

"Let's make a bed for you in the aft storage area," I say, dripping wet again as I drop back into the cabin. "It'll be cramped but dry." And my bunk is too narrow for two.

"Aye, aye, captain," Drew says.

We set about our task, made more difficult by *Sassy* rolling gunwale to gunwale. We keep falling, often crashing into each other. Drew enjoys 'saving' me and the zing of the electrical storm, of surviving it, makes us high-spirited.

Once Drew's lying in the cramped storage space, I hide in the head and change into a dry tank top and the black bikini bottoms I wore on the Trench day. When I emerge, Drew's gaze loiters on my bare legs.

"There's room for a little one here," he shouts over the baying wind.

"I must be at my bunk, just in case." I place the flashlight, alarm, and tools near my pillow. "The storm could return. I need to have my sailing brain switched on. Did you realize I have to wake up every twenty minutes to do safety checks even if the windvane is steering us?"

Drew flops back on his mattress made of spare sails and sleeping bags.

I remember how I craved human contact after a storm during the crossing from California. I feel bad for him. He's had a tough time since he came after me.

I crawl in next to him. "But a few minutes won't hurt."

Drew's arms encircle me, and a long sigh trickles from my throat. He kisses the top of my head. His lips trace down the side of my face, gently stroking, searching. He shifts onto his elbow, and his mouth crushes against mine. I pant. And I kiss him back. The distant storm sends jagged shards of light across the cabin. His kiss deepens, and his palm strokes over my butt and under my tank top to my breast. I shudder and arc into him, make a small mewling sound in the back of my throat, which pulls a moan from him. He clutches me closer. His hand snakes to the ties on my bikini bottoms, but I grip his wrist to make him pause.

Sailing brain.

I use the pause to wriggle away.

I WAKE several times during the night to perform my usual checks. Out on deck, my hair billows, and the waves flog in the dark. The sky swirls like star soup. I re-live our kiss earlier, while my out-of-control body whirls with heat.

I had pulled away from Drew last night because of the need to keep focused, but it was also because I'm falling for him, and that's more frightening than any cyclone.

My sleep is erratic. I toss and turn, knowing if Brett claims the reward, Drew and I will be separated when we dock in Australia. I fitfully dream about being arrested and forcibly dragged away from him. Each time the dream reaches the part where I'm screaming his name, I jump awake.

In the morning, my brain flickers on, and Drew is standing next to my narrow bunk. A golden shaft of light from the porthole spotlights him, his hair tousled, his face still crammed with fatigue.

He stretches his arms out. "Coffee?"

I sit up. "I'll do it."

"Think I can manage a kettle. Let me do *something* around here. Where are we anyway? You could be taking me to visit an island of vampires, and I'd never know." He fills the kettle with water from a bottle, flicks the gas switch, and ignites the stove. On the two-month journey to Samoa, I had often wished someone was there to make a coffee or prepare some food for me.

"We're between Tonga and Fiji, which is clearly nowhere near Vampire Island."

"If you say so, captain. How do you feel today? Did you know you called for me in your sleep?" His grin is triumphant.

I try to forget the dreams that had frightened me and turn my face into the pillow. Drew's fingers stroke my hair. I sit up, pull my knees to me.

He grips the edge of the bunk, his knuckles turning white. "What's up?"

"Maybe it won't be a life sentence, and maybe I will be able to prove it was self-defense, but if Brett snitched, when we reach Australia, I'll still be taken into custody, questioned, charged, deported. They can't say, 'Oh never mind, we know it was self-defense, have a great life.' A man is still dead. There'll be a court case, and I'm probably a flight risk, having already run away once. I'll be in custody the whole time."

"I don't know." He skims my face. "I wish I could answer all your questions. No one's saying it'll be easy, but whatever happens, I'll be there, for however long it takes. And in the end, you will be free to get on with your life. They won't lock you up forever."

But they can if I can't prove Connor was abusive, and I'm not sure I can. "It's my word against a dead man's." I slump onto my side in the bunk, curl into a tight ball.

Drew rubs my arm. "I'm not going anywhere, okay?"

Every part of me wants to feel the way he made me feel last night. But it's not to be. I need to do the right thing.

"I don't want you to put your life on hold for me." He could be waiting for a lifetime. I must push him away. It'd be the same as saving his life. "Drew, I've no intention of having a boyfriend ever again. Not after . . . I'm better on my own."

Surely, he can hear my heart breaking.

The rigging tinkles, metal scrapes on metal in the galley, the waves slosh against the hull, inside a locker, an object rolls and knocks. I never knew how much a person's silence could hurt.

He regards me for the space of a thousand thoughts, then returns to making coffee.

I hadn't meant to sound so harsh. I fumble for the right words. "I think I'm supposed to sail this world alone."

"Only if you choose to."

My chin quivers and tears build. I try a different angle. "I need to protect myself."

"From me? I told you, I'm not Connor."

"I'm not talking about that. I can't let myself . . . it'll hurt too much. If I let you in, I won't know how to let you go when we reach Australia." I grab a pillow and hug it.

Drew takes the pillow and places it aside. "When I was hanging onto the Jesus line and *Sassy* raced off so fast it was impossible to pull myself up the rope, I tied it around myself and spent what seemed forever assuming I wouldn't make it."

"You should've let go. You could've been killed."

181

"That's my point. Letting go was *never* an option." His gaze seizes mine. "And it still isn't."

I fight the impulse to lean forward and kiss him.

"I understand you're afraid of what's going to happen, Shae, and I don't disagree with the protecting yourself from getting hurt part. But for me, whatever happens in Australia, letting you go is not an option." Drew grins. "You can compare me to a dog—loyal to the end."

"If we get in deeper, and I'm arrested . . . Haven't I hurt you enough?"

"So, for all the reasons you've mentioned, we'll keep it just friends. I want you to feel safe with me, too. I want you to believe I'm not like Connor. I won't push anything. I'll wait for you to come to me."

"I won't."

He jerks his chin down and to the side like I just kicked his face. After a stagnant silence, he adds, "We're going to survive all of this." Drew collects my hands. "You're the most courageous person I know. Surviving those weeks at sea— the storms, the doldrums, the sharks. By the sharks, I'm also referring to Brett."

I snort-laugh and blink fiercely against tears. Drew might be right. I may have set out to prove something to my father, even my mother, but in the end, I did it for myself. Now *I know* I'm a survivor.

"I wish you could reach inside me and rip the past out of me," I say. "Erase my memory."

"Then you wouldn't be the person you are now. And I really like that person."

Everything I need to know is in his smile.

But given how he's cradling me with his eyes, how will we survive being pulled apart?

CHAPTER 25

I spend the rest of that day teaching Drew the basics of sailing. By sundown, he's doing a good job going solo. He hadn't so much as put a glance out of line, and I feel relaxed. It had been a perfect day.

While sitting at the bow of *Sassy*, we glide into the crimson sunset. Our legs dangle over the parting waves and the wind blasts the hair off our faces so our smiles seem bigger. When night curls around us, we soar through the dark as if we're the only ones left on Earth.

It's too hot to sleep in the cabin, so we pull a mattress and pillows into the cockpit and settle under the glow of a lantern and *Sassy*'s external lights. We lie on our backs, arms pressed together, watching for shooting stars.

My heart unfurls, luffs like a wayward sail. *Pretend he's a brother.*

"Tell me about Brett when he was a kid," I say.

Drew tosses a handful of beef jerky into his mouth, grinds his jaw. "He was great to escape with. We hung outside and the branches of a jacaranda tree became an underground train, a wattle tree was a flying castle, or the pathway between our houses was a trench in World War Six against the aliens. Brett totally believed it, as if it wasn't a game. He was intense but in a good way."

"When did he change?"

"Around thirteen. He started getting into trouble at school. Drinking, stealing. Guess he was acting out. His father had remarried when Brett was seven and barely acknowledged him. Brett had already been abandoned by his mother when he was a baby and after the re-marriage, he felt as if he wasn't wanted at home, especially after his dad had three more kids with his new wife. I had no idea what he was up to when he wasn't with me until one day, he pushed me into taking the rap for his shoplifting. He said if his father found out, he'd be disinherited. His dad was always threatening to do that."

"Why'd he shoplift if he knew that would happen?"

"I don't know. I'm sure a psychologist would have the answers." He passes me the jerky.

"You keep saying Brett's story isn't yours to tell. But I need to understand how it is that he attacked me, yet you still haven't ended the friendship. How can you stand by a man like that?"

Drew pinches the bridge of his nose. "I guess it does seem odd. Sorry. I hadn't realized how it would look to you." Drew puts down the jerky and sinks lower on the mattress. "Ever hear of John Paul Getty III?" I shake my head. "Brett's story is a weird modern-day copycat of Getty's story. Brett's father was always threatening to disinherit Brett, and Brett would joke that he was going to stage his own kidnapping so it wouldn't matter. But then Brett *was* kidnapped. For real. For a $10 million-dollar ransom."

"Jeez. His parents really are loaded?"

"His father's a celebrity lawyer. So, he's famous, too. Anyway, of course his father thought it was a joke and refused to pay the money. He told the press and the police about Brett's threats to stage a kidnapping and they believed him. He also said he'd never pay a ransom because if he did, that would put his three daughters' lives at risk because they'd be kidnapped next. Brett was held in a basement for months where they treated him like an animal. Not enough food, sleeping on a thin yoga mat, and a bucket for a toilet. They told him his father refused to pay. Let's just say it reinforced Brett's belief he wasn't wanted or loved."

"That would really mess someone up. I can see what you mean. How did he escape?"

"In Getty's case, the kidnappers posted his ear to his parents to prove it was a genuine kidnapping. But Brett convinced the kidnappers to take his finger instead, and to post it to me because his father would probably throw it away, which I'm sure he wouldn't have. But Brett wasn't risking it."

"So, you got the finger?"

"Yeah. Nice gift from the postman. My father stepped in and convinced Brett's dad to pay up. Our fathers never did get on so I've no idea how he managed that. Brett was dumped at a school playground."

We lapse into silence, and I lie flatter on the mattress to watch the night sky. I work through the ordeal Brett had been through, finally understanding why Drew couldn't give up on him. Possibly that showed Drew wouldn't give up on me, either.

Smiling at him now, I step off the spinning merry-go-round of my thoughts and into the calm, steady gaze of Drew. I've never felt so safe or close to anyone, not in the kissing sense, but in the sense of truly trusting each other.

That night, our words and laughter hover in the soft air until we float into sleep.

———

ONE DAY SHUFFLES into the next and the next. When Drew

isn't sailing, he idles away time by sketching. At first, he's frustrated by the lack of colored pencils aboard, so he can't draw the magical twilights. But he soon fills a notebook with sketches of me—at the helm, relaxing on the gunwale, scrubbing down *Sassy*, studying charts at the nav table, hanging up washed clothes. Dolphins, sea eagles, and stingrays visit, and he illustrates them while leaning against the mast.

The first time a squall finds us, I show him how to take a freshwater shower. He shampoos his hair and sticks his head in a bucket to rinse, shaking off and spraying me when he's done. Shirtless, his shorts held up by a rope belt, he's a Robinson Crusoe look-a-like.

And no matter what he's doing, I watch him. Ache for him.

"Breakfast," Drew announces. He's taken on the role of head chef since I am captain. Sitting together in the cockpit, he places the plate on my lap.

"You figured out the powdered eggs," I tease.

"I'm no chef, but boat food has good instructions. If I can read, I can cook."

We scoop up mouthfuls of scrambled eggs but both snort, mid-chew.

I gulp. "Why do you have mixed raisins in here?"

He laughs and pokes at the raisins with his fork. "I thought they were bacon bits."

"Ha. You'll be lucky to find anything resembling bacon around here."

"Good thing you're a better captain than I am a chef." He puts his plate aside and focuses on my bikini. "Can't we go for a swim?"

"Sharks? Not so much fun if your boat sails off without you, either."

Drew grabs a bucket from the well of the cockpit and leans over the gunwale, lowering it by its rope into the ocean. "I'll just have to get us wet another way."

"Don't even think about it." I clamber away from him.

"Thought about it. Doing it." Drew gives chase and lobs the water at me.

Using the empty dishwashing bucket, I retaliate, and we get stuck into a serious water fight, jostling all over *Sassy*. Drew wins when he snatches my bucket and double dumps me. The whole time I know the game is an excuse to touch each other and between the jokes and laughter are waves of longing.

DREW LEANS AGAINST THE MAST, sketching, as I helm *Sassy*. Content, I watch the cryptic reflections of scrappy clouds in the tranquil sea. Suddenly, I jolt forward. The wheel wrenches out of my grip. A scratchy noise emanates from underneath *Sassy*. Drew joins me in the cockpit. I yank at the helm. It's sticky, and the sails flag. *Sassy* jerks and inadvertently changes direction. *Stay focused.* I can hear my father's instructions to remain calm so my brain has space to think. As he'd taught me, I go through the options one by one. *Be logical but quick.* I furl the sails, heave to, and lay anchor.

"Is everything okay?" Drew asks once I stand still again.

"Something's wrong under the boat." I lean over the aft and glare into the water. A knot of rope surrounds the rudder. *Sassy* rises and falls, and the movement reveals a crab pot covered in strings of kelp. *There's a crab pot wrapped around the rudder.* With nothing aboard to hook the rope or to push it off, the situation seems hopeless.

Go in the water and untangle it. A solo sailor should never leave the boat. That's the first rule of solo sailing. But I must free the rudder. Without steering, we're going nowhere. We can't stay here stranded, waiting for the police to catch up, waiting for a cyclone to take us out.

"What can you see?" Drew asks.

"There's a rope from a crab pot wrapped around our rudder." I drop below and snatch up a deck knife. I clip myself to the boat, fingers trembling, and tell myself it's a calm day, and *Sassy* shouldn't abruptly shift and whack me on the skull, knocking me out—or worse, kill me.

"You're not going in," Drew states. "You said there were sharks."

An image of a shark's fin and the music from *Jaws* side-swipes me. "I have no choice. We can't go anywhere until the rope's cut away."

"Let me do it then."

I step onto the gunwale, checking and re-checking my safety harness. *Don't drop the knife.*

Drew grabs my hand. "Seriously, I'm not letting you go in."

"I've watched Finn and my dad do this. I won't be told what I can and can't do. There's no choice, and I'm not going to toss for which of us takes this risk. I'm doing it. I know what I'm doing, you don't."

Still looking unhappy, Drew drops my hand. I drag in a huge breath and jump over the side of the boat, clutching the blade, and thinking I should've brought a spare or tied it to my wrist.

When I tug at the tangled rope, it only tightens the knots. I come up for air, ignoring the possibility of what might be swimming underneath me. The seawater stings my eyes, but I hack at the ropes and every thirty seconds, I swim back up to breathe. *Sassy*'s position keeps changing so I duck under and move the rudder with my hands to keep us upwind.

Something touches my foot. The sound of my underwater scream distorts. I choke on seawater, but there's nothing below except the swirling kelp around the crab pot.

"What happened?" Drew's concerned face hovers above me.

"Just the kelp touched me. I got scared."

"Let me take a turn. Have a break."

"No. I need to ensure *Sassy*'s upwind. It's complicated. I'll be fine."

After a million minutes, my arm muscles and lungs are burning. The next time I dive, I'm ferocious with the knife strokes. But there are too many loops to cut through and the rudder keeps bashing into me. Fear enters me like a thousand worms. I squash them. *Just do it.* I transform into a mutant octopus and hack, thrust, slash, and slice at the ropes. I rise to gulp for air often, choking on strands of hair that stick to my face.

A century later, it comes free. I guide the crab pot away, ensuring any remaining rope doesn't give me a repeat of the whole catastrophe. I watch it float a few meters adrift before dragging myself on board.

"You did it," Drew yells, wrapping me in a hug. "But jeez, you gave me a fright. My heart feels as if it's been boxed like a speed ball. I think you deserve a reward. Roast chicken and spuds? A hot shower? A glass of wine? Sit by a crackling fire?" He reels off some other ideas, none of which are possibilities.

Instead, I lean in and kiss him gently on the lips. "I'll have to settle for one single kiss." A flare goes off inside me.

THE PINK and orange sunset is dappled with unusual pockets of gold and turquoise. The sea reflects the sky and evolves into a molten vista of swaying pinks and yellows. There isn't an up or a down, and we could be in the middle of a pot of melting marshmallows. And when night whips in, *Sassy*'s lights transform the ocean spray into sparklers against the dark rollers.

Drew and I settle at the bow, or as Drew calls it, to get a reaction, the *pointy end* of *Sassy*. It's our favorite spot on the boat. We grin into the black breeze.

"How long have we been at sea?" Drew re-ties the lace on his swimming trunks.

I turn my stare away from his bare chest. "Thirteen days."

"I'll make pancakes and jam for breakfast in the morning, if you want."

The suggestion makes me jolt, then bristle. I try to hold in the words, but they flare into the space between us anyway. "No. No pancakes."

"Because?"

"Because you know why. It's too close a reminder. I don't want to go there."

"That's exactly why you should. You shouldn't block out the good memories of your father."

"Says Mr. Psychiatrist who can't even work out why Brett steals when he knows it'll get him disinherited." I pull myself up on the lifelines, a familiar mix of anger and guilt boiling over. I hear Drew follow and wish *Sassy* had more than one cabin, more than thirty-four feet to her.

He plunks next to me in the well of the cockpit. "Sorry if I pushed a button. I'm being a know-it-all, aren't I?" I exhale and shrug. He slips an arm around my shoulders. "I'd hate for you to make the same mistakes I made, that's all."

Craving comfort, I lean into him. "What do you mean?"

"I was furious with my mom for working too hard and never having any time for me and then it was too late. She died. And there was no more time left. And it seemed to me that she'd chosen to leave me. The only thing left was my anger. Instead of mourning her, I got angrier and blocked out our memories. It took a long time, but I figured out the anger was eating away at me. I felt so much better after I let it go and let myself remember all the good moments."

Still leaning into Drew, I pull up my knees.

He tugs me closer. "Anger's normal. It's okay to feel it— just not forever. For your own sake. You have to forgive everyone, including yourself, and let the anger go so it doesn't affect you for the rest of your life."

"The difference is my dad became a monster, beat up my mother, he . . ."

I consider how I'd been thinking of my father during this whole crossing. He'd helped me. Each time I needed to get over an obstacle, fight a fear, or survive a storm, his voice was in my mind, guiding me. There were so many good times. And I remember his letters and how it was anger that fed the monster inside him. Hadn't I intended to give Finn the letters to help him let go of his own anger?

"You're right." A rush of tears overtake my words.

Drew rubs up and down my spine, ruching my tank top with each stroke. He snakes a pinkie around my little finger. "Hey, come on," he says. I'm shaking under his touch. "You need time. It's a cliché for a reason." I crush my face into him. He tugs at my pinkie. "And I'm here to help." His words are breathy, not a whisper, but more of a thought spoken aloud by mistake. He strokes my hair and my back, then pulls me down with him so we're lying on the mattress on the cockpit floor. Calmer now, I let him console me and I get lost in him, rising and sinking as we breathe together.

"I'm sorry," he says after a while. "I don't ever want to upset you." He pulls one of my legs across his, and we still fit each other. His fingers trail down my face and neck, his breathing ragged. I draw comfort from the heat of him and after a while, he sings.

The melody rolls through the night air, taking me back to the fire-lit beach on Samoa. His voice, the touch of his skin against mine, the coconut and sunshine smell of him. I want to cling to him forever and never let go.

When he finishes, I tilt my face up to request another song.

His burning eyes make my request vanish into the night.

He shifts to his elbow. I push my lips onto his. His hand cradles my head. He kisses my mouth open, and I let him in. The kiss is slow and loving and reduces the pace of my heart to a notch above stop.

He breaks from my mouth and kisses my neck. Gentle. Relaxed. Like leisurely plucking the chords on a guitar. Urging aside my tank top and bikini straps from my shoulders, his lips trail across my shoulder and up to the line of my jaw. Stretched with my need for him after so many days of denial, I move my mouth to his and our tongues rally. His fingertips trace from my brow, over my cheekbones, and to our joined mouths. The touch of his fingers on my mouth is intense and sets off a blissful pull of muscles deep inside me. But then Drew retreats and lies on his back again, bringing me sideways with him. My insides still purr and curl like twisting smoke.

"We mustn't," he whispers. He thumbs at my frown.

I watch his words bob and scuttle away as he tries to explain. "Believe me, there's nothing I want more." My breath shudders. "I want us to be perfect in every way, but you said—"

"I don't want to wait anymore." I think about how, if I'm sent down for life, I'll never make love to Drew.

We map each other's faces.

I sit and pull my tank top over my head, then reach behind to unfasten my bikini top. It drops away, and I feel my nipples tighten in the breeze. Drew, still watching my face, brushes a nipple with his thumb. I lean into him to grab his mouth with mine, then lay on him, skin to skin. He kisses me, fierce yet tender, and I let his warm hands roam over my naked back and under my bikini bottoms to rest on my butt cheeks. One hand stays there, and the other drifts up my body, grazing the delicate skin of my waist and the edge of my breast. I wait for him to remove the rest of my bikini and his trunks, but he's in no rush. He seems content to simply feel every part of my exposed skin while exploring every part of my mouth with his tongue.

He bites my bottom lip and sucks it, then nuzzles my neck, slipping his hands between us to caress my breasts. I feel his hardness against my leg, and I shift and press myself against him. An ache opens between my legs, and I want to feel his weight on me, want to fill the hot hollowness inside me. I roll to my side and bring him on top, spreading my legs so he lays between them. He holds me tight and kisses me deeper and harder until we're both panting. When he raises himself to circle my nipples with his tongue, he pulls at the strings to release my bikini bottoms, then traces down over my belly and into the moistness between my legs. His tongue continues to dance and suck until I'm bucking and gasping. I had never felt the full power of an orgasm, only the edges of one.

I'm still drifting in my bliss when I feel Drew's body settle against mine, and then the pressure of him entering me. My breath hitches and I pant as he moves within me, wallowing in streaks of ecstatic sensation. I relax and widen my legs, open my mouth to his probing tongue, and let go of everything but Drew.

AFTER THAT NIGHT, we can't keep our hands off each other— an arm squeeze in passing, a slap after a cheeky comment, standing arm in arm to watch a pod of dolphins, lazing in the circle of Drew's legs as he leans on the mast, entwining pinkies while we watch the distant storms. We're busy with sailing and cleaning and repairs during the day, so the touching tides us over until the night when we lie together and talk for hours and make love—slow, sensual, tender, as if we have all the time in the world. I have never felt freer. Or happier.

But it doesn't last.

One afternoon, a plane flies overhead. It's a reminder we're closing in on civilization. The sight of it crams fear into me—it's flying low and could have identified us.

CHAPTER 26

"I could get used to this sailing life." Drew beams as he helms us through the turquoise waters. The sails run wing and wing, and we resemble a giant dove coming in to land on the water. He loves the speed as twelve knots of wind thrust us forward.

The sun creates dancing sparkles on the crests of the choppy waves. From the cockpit, I squint into the glare and wash the lunch plates in a bucket of rainwater. Our only worry during the last week was the diminishing supply of drinking water—with Drew on board, we're going through it twice as fast. But he stepped up and built a makeshift bowl out of a spare sail, and it's capturing fresh rain in the squalls so effectively the problem is solved.

A sailor in his own right now, I watch him as he works around the boat, shirtless and sure-footed.

"We should give Australia a miss and sail the world for the rest of our lives," he says.

I flick water at him, and he gifts me with my favorite smile, the one that says a million intimate things in just one look.

"It'd be impossible," I say. "Because you're too similar to

Finn. Way too messy and terrible at washing dishes. At least you don't spend hours in the head like Mom used to."

We slip into a snug silence. Eventually, I add, "We'd run out of money and supplies, or *Sassy* would need repairs or be capsized one too many times. And we'd always be tense with the fear of being caught."

Drew laughs as he works a winch. "You've been giving this some thought then."

"Only on a few occasions . . . per hour," I say, and his smile takes over his face.

We bask in the freedom and the placid weather and when the nights cool as we approach Australia, because it's winter there, we zip together two sleeping bags in the cockpit. And each time I'm on watch, I watch Drew more than the horizon.

I think of my family more and more. Will they believe me when I tell them what happened? My mother had put up with the violence, but she never fought back. Will she judge me or understand? I want them to see my father's letters, too. Over the past few weeks since I read them, I've slowly let go of the rage I had nurtured against him. I want that for Finn and my mother so they can move forward with their lives.

———

I POINT out constellations as Drew and I lie staring at the stars with linked pinkies. "They seem closer and brighter out here," I say. I've taught Drew how to identify and name them so he can use the sextant to navigate. Then I add the words I've kept hidden. "It's been twenty days. We're about three days from Townsville."

We lie in silence, my chest packed with the breath I can't seem to let out.

THE NEXT MORNING, a spray of water washes across us and we jump awake under building purplish, gray clouds and a fluky wind.

"Honeymoon's over, honey," Drew jokes.

"I believe that's called being 'pooped on' in the sailing world."

We throw our makeshift bed below and slog to adjust the sails. In the cabin, a locker busts open and spills its contents. We work to confine everything that can be locked down or put away to avoid flying lethal weapons. We had been slacking during the calm weather, and the cabin is a mess. I had also extended the twenty-minute checks lately, so now the weather's woken us, we're behind in our preparation for a storm. Fear jumps to attention inside me, and I snap my sailing brain on.

The wind gauge reads twenty-two knots and rising. The bleating wind and the walls of waves hike sharply. My nerves jangle while *Sassy* moans and joggles after a gust at thirty knots. Up on deck, Drew works the winches, looking excited, as if he's about to go on a rollercoaster. But I've seen the radar, and I am not quite so thrilled. I set up a drogue, the parachute-like device that slows our descent down steep waves. We stay above until the wind whips so hard the rain's like a steel-tipped comb aggravating our skin, driving us below.

"We're inside a cork, bobbing on the ocean," Drew says as we're shoved left, then right.

The sea becomes a many-spined monster, and the wind hits an almighty fifty knots. We brace each time *Sassy* surfs walls of water the size of three-story apartment buildings. Even Drew lets out a shout of both shock and exhilaration. I've done this before—a few times between California and Samoa—and I can only trust *Sassy* will save us once again.

The wind changes from a constant roar to a prolonged scream, and the ocean sends its biggest train of waves. *Sassy* is hoisted up, slammed sideways. We're both bashed against the bulkhead above the bunk. A locker flies open, dumps its contents. A steel flashlight narrowly misses my cheek. *Sassy* groans and lies on her side, a wounded horse. I guess the mast is all but in the water.

"Come on, *Sassy*. Up you get," I yell. Drew's eyebrow is gashed and bloody. "Are you okay? What hit you?"

"Flying screwdriver." He rolls his eyes, but they're looped with apprehension, probably thinking what I'm thinking—why worry what'll happen when we reach Australia, when we probably won't make it there at all?

Sassy pulls upright. In the short reprieves between the end of one wave and the start of another, Drew and I shoot around securing the cabin, and I clean up Drew's graze. At midnight, the wind falls to twenty-five knots, and we catnap—me in my bunk, Drew in his sleeping hole. A cracking roar so loud I truly believe an airplane is about to crash into *Sassy* wakes us. I'm lying on the side of the bulkhead, the mast past ninety degrees. We hang there for a moment.

"Shae." Drew's voice carves through the darkness.

"I'm okay. You okay?"

"I can't believe you did this on your own. You are one hell of a ballsy chick."

I laugh nervously.

Sassy shakes herself off, and we're upright again. Forty-three knots, four in the morning, and back to surfing apartment block-high waves. We strap ourselves in and pass a box of dry cereal between us. Watching the radar, it's a bigger setback than I let on. George's worries about cyclone season have materialized.

We ride the gales through daybreak and for a few more hours, it's as if the waves are being shot from a cannon.

"I win the largest bruise competition," Drew jokes. I know he'd rather be asking, *are we going to die?*

"Check this out." I lift the back of my T-shirt. A bruise the size of a dinner plate looms.

"Okay, you win. But I'm working on beating you."

Hours later, a mutinous wind provides a second's warning. We catch each other's glance. A roaring ogre of a wave approaches on the starboard side. Through the porthole, it's a wall of water without edges. Despite my death grip on the handholds, my back slams into the bulkhead. I might have blacked out for a moment. I find myself resting on the ceiling, Drew beside me, being showered by clothes, batteries, cutlery, a frying pan, bottles of water, and cans of food like bullets being fired at us. And then water from the bilge dumps on us.

The cabin is darker than usual, the sound of the storm muffled.

Sassy takes on an eeriness that scares me.

Drew sits and the cabin brightens—he'd been lying on the cabin light. But with the portholes submerged underwater, the glow is a dull, creepy green.

And *Sassy* isn't popping up.

"We're rolling," I yell in disbelief. Our bodies crash down the opposite bulkhead. With nothing to grab onto, we collide into each other and land in what could be a paddling pool of water. "That was a three-sixty roll. The mast has to be gone."

Like a branch against a windowpane, something spiky scrapes above us.

"You can't go out there now," Drew commands.

"In a minute, I have to." We brace for another wave, skid down the front of it.

In the short lull, Drew takes my elbow. "You'll die. This storm isn't kidding around."

"If the mast is broken, it could damage our hull and we'll sink." I grab my harness. "Then we *both* definitely die. And it's better if I don't have to worry about two of us up there."

"I know you hate relying on anyone but yourself, but

there's no way I'm letting you go up there to risk your life for me."

I slam my mouth shut on the words I want to say and pass him his harness, then grab the deck knives. I understand his need to help, and he is a sailor in his own right. We step gingerly through the hatch, squinting through the whirling rain. The broken boom sticks out of the cockpit, a giant pencil in a pencil cup. It's leaning on a busted windvane. The fifty-foot mast is in the ocean, the end resting on the edge of the deck, attached to *Sassy* by shrouds and tangled lines. Only a stump remains. With no chance of lashing together a temporary mast and no engine, it means we're stranded. We could drift for weeks.

We may never be found.

CHAPTER 27

"Cut the lines to free the mast," I shout over the wind. Drew cups his ear. I grab a line and make cutting motions with my hands. We hack while the ocean pummels *Sassy*, and clutch anything we can reach when the wave jacks up. It's as if we're on a thirty-four-foot surfboard. In the back of my mind is the terrifying possibility we could capsize while on deck, be knocked unconscious or pinned under the boat. I concentrate on cutting the shrouds. At least we have daylight on our side.

Drew has his rollercoaster ride except we're perched on *top* of the car, and we don't only rise and fall and dive but are randomly side-jerked and forced to balance at ridiculous angles with water dumping over us. Drew sticks to his task, even though most beginners would huddle in a corner of the cabin.

Without the windvane, *Sassy* moves side-on to the waves. The risk of being knocked down and rolling again increases. I smother the fear, like putting a blanket over the cage of a squawking parrot to quieten it. Through the screaming wind, I indicate to Drew that I'm going to the helm. He knows enough to grasp that we must surf square-on to the waves. Flicking his hair to clear his vision, he continues to hack at the lines.

A wild stallion of a wave rears up, and we tumble sideways down a cliff-face of water. I'm flung against the lifelines, but Drew drops off the vertical cabin roof and flies into the raging ocean.

"*Drew! Drew!*" The sea is a boiling mass of battleship-gray water and white foam. As *Sassy* rights herself, I struggle to find him through the curtain of rain.

His head pops up.

He's holding onto the mast, which is a floating log attached to the boat by one line. *Sassy* could land on him or the mast might knock him out. He pulls himself up by his harness, but the ocean heaves, too powerful, and he can only get so far before it pounds him backward.

Sassy surges up the front of a wave and down again. The mast hits Drew between his shoulder blades. He arches as if someone shot him. Frantic, I hack at the remaining shroud. Water lashes into my face and it's hard to tell the difference between the drenching rain, the gushing waves, and my tears of fear. The mast finally falls away.

The rumble of another giant breaker makes me twist round and scream. The wave jacks up, higher and higher, a tower of water. It collapses, flogs my body like dozens of whips, so hard I'm flattened onto the boat and flicked into the sea, a broken ragdoll. Unable to bring air into my lungs, I clutch at my ribs and take in sips of air. I circle my legs to keep my face above water, but each time my harness tugs, fiery pain crackles through me.

The ocean has finally won.

Something pulls and all at once, Drew has me. We rise and fall, ten meters from *Sassy*. His arm holds me around the waist. The pain nearly makes me pass out.

"You have to get aboard," I shout-wince.

"I'm not letting you go."

"If you don't, we'll both die. My ribs . . . I'm injured."

Drew grasps my harness and tries to pull us both forward. It's slow progress, and we're clobbered back by the next wave. He fails repeatedly and must know he's out of choices.

He rests his lips on my temple, holds them there for a long moment. I feel the heat of his breath as he breathes me in.

Then he lets me go.

A swell lifts us, propelling us apart.

I float when possible or sink under to avoid the peak of the waves pushing me down. Gritting my teeth against the pain, I'm close to losing consciousness.

But this can't be the end for me and Drew.

Time passes in a gray and white roaring blur. The swells shrink and the wind becomes less boisterous. I'm shivering with cold. I kick to turn around and hunt for Drew, expecting him to be floating on the surface in order to stay above water, exhausted. But I'm so wrong. He's a one-man advancing army, surging forward, being forced back, and surging forward again. He never takes his focus off the target —*Sassy Jam*.

I recognize something I have known yet have never seen, like watching a falling star for the first time. His love for me pushes Drew now, driving him, under no circumstances allowing him to be defeated. He will never give up. *As I know I won't—for his sake.*

I've come to believe that falling in love somehow weakens you, makes you half of a person and turns you into someone's Play-Doh. Now, I understand true love can make you do things you never believed possible. It can empower you.

203

AM I DEAD?

When I open my eyes, it's dark and still and silent. I try to sit but cry out in pain.

"Shae, don't move." Drew's rock-solid voice infuses relief into every part of me. *Unless he's dead, too.*

A yellow light flicks on, and Drew is there. His smile fills me with sunshine. It seems the place I once longed to sail to, the bliss I thought was on the other side of the sunset, is no longer somewhere out there, but right here inside me. I reach to touch him.

He squeezes my hand. "Hey."

"Hey." I'm smiling like a complete idiot. "You made it. You didn't give up."

He touches my cheek. "Never."

I take in a breath, but wince with pain.

"Does it hurt to breathe? You might've broken some ribs."

"*Everything* hurts. Was I asleep long?"

"Few hours." He punctures tablets from their foil. "Painkillers." He pops two in my mouth, lifts my head to sip from a bottle. "You went out cold before I could give them to you."

He's wearing the shorts from the beach party, and his torso is patterned with bruises and scrapes. "Are you injured?" I ask.

"Feel like I've done ten rounds with an army of angry gorillas."

We laugh but then grimace with pain, which makes us laugh more.

Despite everything, happiness balloons inside me.

Our eyes cling. We don't need words because love is written all over our faces, bursting from our smiles, sparkling in our eyes, and it's a moment more intimate than any kiss we've ever shared.

I command myself to focus on the movement of the boat. "It's so quiet without the rigging. What time is it?"

"Ten-thirty at night. Storm's gone. Hardly any wind."

"We lost the mast."

Drew nods. "Just us inside a bubble, bobbing about on the ocean." He bends to kiss my nose, maybe believing it's the only part of me that doesn't hurt.

I hold his arms so he must stay leaning close. "No tinkling of the rigging. It's as if *Sassy* can't talk to me anymore," I say.

His gaze combs my face, and I thumb his lip, kiss the spot I thumbed. He glows as if I put a rainbow inside him.

After a while, he straightens and clears his throat. "I'm drying out the stove. It got so wet it won't light. Hopefully it'll dry, and we can have a hot drink. Don't know about you, but I swallowed that much ocean it's as if it washed me both inside and out. Reckon the salt content in my blood is at dangerous levels."

"Can I have some more water?"

Drew turns to fetch it and there's a circular wound on his back. It's swollen and red and purple, resembling a mini backpack where the mast bashed him. He brings another blanket with the water. After he's laid it over me, he takes my hand again, his expression grave. "We'll heal. Guess we can't sail on forever now."

"Nope. That little dream is gone."

I don't mention that I have no clue if we'll ever see land again. At this point, *Sassy Jam* is nothing more than a floating coffin.

CHAPTER 28

When the sun rises, I leverage myself from under at least three blankets. Drew's out cold in his sleeping hole. I pop more tablets and inch through stabbing rib pain toward the navigation table. None of the electrical equipment works—no radar, wind instruments, AIS, radio. I write a list of action points.

Set off the EPIRB
Determine current position
Find flare gun
Find something to build a jury-rig with
Dry out the cabin, clothes, bedding, plus tidy up
Check water and food—ration it
Get stove working

The list is something my father would do. A survival plan.

I shiver, needing dry, warmer clothes, but the cabin is a bomb-wreck. *Six-thirty in the morning and freezing. Where are we?* Moving at a snail's pace, I bring the sextant and open the companionway hatch. The fresh breeze gives me goose bumps. I can't believe this restful ocean, gray now due to thick, low clouds, once beat us so viciously. Not only is *Sassy* de-masted, her sails lost at sea like a queen de-throned, but most of the lifelines are bent or missing, the solar panels battered, and the wind generator has vanished . . . and we'll be out of power soon. We need to hunt down every flashlight and lantern after I've confirmed our position so a tanker doesn't take us out.

Drew emerges from below. He flops next to me on the bench seat and grimaces. "I feel as if I'm 580 years old. Why are you out of your bunk?"

"We've got a lot to do," I say.

"I saw your list. What's an EPIRB?"

"An emergency beacon. When you set it off, the emergency services can determine your position. But only if my father registered it. If he didn't, it won't work."

"Okay. You do that. I'll do everything else. I don't have broken ribs."

"*Possible* broken ribs. Maybe I'm only badly bruised."

"And maybe I'm a sack of potatoes. Talking of which, I could eat a horde of stampeding wildebeest." He disappears below and emerges with dried bananas, tinned potatoes, and tinned mackerel. "Quick, before it's rationed."

Shivering in my damp bikini and shorts, I force down a handful of banana chips. "It's cold. Perhaps we're headed for the south pole. I should finish plotting our position."

I get to work with the sextant and then I make some rapid calculations in the cabin. "We've kept going west thanks to the east-west current," I shout up the stairs. "We're only ninety miles from the Australian east coast. Closer to Brisbane than Townsville though."

Drew approaches to inspect the maps over my shoulder. "It's still winter in Australia. We should dry some warmer clothes. The night temperatures can fall to fifty degrees."

Somehow encouraged, we set about completing our list.

The EPIRB shows no signs of life and is probably not

even connected. The radio is a dead lump of steel. Drew hangs sodden garments on a makeshift wash line, transforming the cabin into a humid steam room because there are no lines outside. I search for something to make a temporary mast with but find nothing, though Drew does find the flare gun inside a pot.

Drew insists on binding a bandage around my ribs. "Checked the food," he says. "Got enough to last months, and we can collect water. We shouldn't use the bottled water for washing anymore." He lightly taps my ribs, the job done. "We could be drifting for weeks."

Neither of us adds, *or months* or *until we run out of food and water and die.*

The cockpit is the driest place onboard, and we make our bed there, despite the chill in the air. With our various injuries, Drew lies on his side. and I need to be on my back. He laces his fingers through mine. I check the tell-tale ribbon now tied to a lifeline—the prevailing wind is still due west. High in the early evening sky, a full moon warms into a golden orb.

"What's the first food you're going to eat when we get ashore?" Drew asks.

I chuckle. "A hunk of pork in coconut sauce?"

"Might have to go back to Samoa for that." He tweaks my nose, amusement dancing in his eyes. "I'll take a steak and a plate of hot, salty chips."

"Apples, waffles with maple syrup, and fried eggs."

"Hot croissants, real coffee, and eggplant," Drew shouts, as if ordering home delivery.

"Eggplant?"

"What? I love barbecued eggplant."

I squeeze his hand and turn my face to him.

Drew's gaze settles in mine. "It'll be okay," he whispers.

"What will you say to your dad when you see him?"

"Thirteen months since I was home . . ." He focuses on

something behind me. "Depends on what happens to you. But after all this," he flicks his chin at where the mast should be, "and after everything you've been through, even if he disowns me, I'll survive." His jaw clenches.

I press my lips to his and, beyond exhausted, we fall asleep in our floating coffin, hand in hand, almost nose to nose, unsure if the wind will change direction and send us who knows where.

AN UNFAMILIAR ROAR WAKES US.

Alarmed, we struggle to sit. I scan for a rogue wave even though the ocean is calm. But the sound is coming from the sky. Drew fetches a red towel and waves it. The plane flies over *Sassy* before he can fetch the flare gun.

Drew pushes rigid fingers through his hair. "They must have seen something."

THE NEXT DAY, Drew sketches while I skim the sky for storms and try to think of any other options for us. With only a light wind, we loll over a never-ending conveyor belt of swells. The concept of doing this for months is daunting yet tolerable, but I'm fighting to forget the other possibilities —of never being found, of watching each other die, of a storm sending us to the bottom of the sea.

"I've got some drawings for you to keep," Drew says, finishing off another one.

"To pin to a prison wall," I say with tears in my voice.

He slips into the cockpit where I'm sitting and holds me. He's dropped the pencil sketch onto the wet deck, one of me at the bow of *Sassy*, my hair flurrying behind. Water darkens the paper, making the image ebb away.

We hear the rumbling noise at the same time. I scan for lightning.

"A plane." I scramble to let off a flare, this time kept close by. Drew mounts the cabin roof with the red towel. When we spot the orange propeller plane with the words *Rescue* on the side, we wave and holler. It flies over *Sassy Jam* and circles back, dipping its wings before flying off in the direction it came. *They've found us.*

Drew leaps off the roof and hugs me. "No more doom and gloom. It's going to be fine." He presses his lips to mine. "Reckon we've got one more night. It's too late to attempt a rescue now."

It's a moment of joy quickly eclipsed by the shiver of reality, the fear of what's to come, a sense of something collapsing inside me.

I watch the moon, and it watches us. I like that it's solely the three of us in the world—me, Drew, and *Sassy*.

Excitement about being rescued is part of why I can't sleep, but tomorrow is the first day of the rest of my life. I'm so close to seeing my family, to facing the justice system, the media, separating from Drew.

The thoughts stack up inside me until I'm being choked.

How do I get used to a world without Drew—to never being bathed in sunshine? How will I cope without him filling me with light and possibility every day, with never curling up inside his gaze, for my heart to never feel so stunned with love? How will I keep him fresh in my memory, so alive and clear that just his memory is enough? Maybe forever.

I shoot upright. My breath comes in solid hunks.

Drew slips his arm around me. Rays of moonlight poke

through the cloud like torches from heaven—despite the beauty surrounding us, the core of me is coming undone.

"What if this is our last night ever?" I ask.

"I promise you it's not."

Drew encourages me to lie down with him. Our heads share a single pillow. When Drew kisses me, my body hums, and I'm almost certain my tears mingle with his. I kiss him back fiercely, as if he holds my last breath inside his throat.

CHAPTER 29

As soon as I register the brightness behind my eyelids, an invisible fist grips me. Overwhelming regret and fear rush from my toes right out the top of my head. My stomach wrings itself out. It's almost intolerable.

Drew's awake, watching me. His hand covers mine.

"Why isn't there an option to switch off the sun?" I whisper. By the angle of the sun, it's much later than when we normally wake.

"A pause button would be good."

We ransack each other's eyes, trying to say everything we feel without words because there aren't words big enough. There must be a way to stop time, turn it back, set it to repeat.

Repeat, repeat.

Our kiss is deep, gentle, as if we have all the time in the world. But still the kiss is too brief, and Drew leaves me too soon, and the heat of him in the sleeping bag cools too quickly. I can hardly bear it.

We're clearing up breakfast in the galley when the porthole frames the Search & Rescue boat. Reality gouges me.

The floor stirs and whooshes beneath my feet. *If only we could run away.*

On deck, I grab Drew and he grabs me, aware time is unraveling at a breakneck pace and can't be clawed back. My pulse zips and my throat closes. Drew's breathing is unstitched, his features tense with too many emotions.

He turns to me and cups my face in both his hands. "From the moment I watched you drink coconut milk off that plate at the fish market . . . Never forget, I love you, Shae."

The look on his face is freshly cut love.

The world hushes, stills, as if it's on hold. Perhaps it is possible to pause time for a while.

I half-sob and drop my forehead on his chest. I desperately want to say it back, but the words are buried too deep inside me. The last time I said them to Connor, I lived to regret giving them away so freely. And now the words hold too much hope. What if I never see Drew again?

"I wish I could take this from you, take the rap," he adds. "But whatever happens, I'll wait for you." We remain knotted together, swaying with *Sassy*. Drew's eyes are jammed with unshed tears.

The SAR boat pulls closer. A line of four orange-clad men grin at us. "Ahoy there."

We wave and shout back from twenty meters apart.

I scan for policemen. Behind the SAR guys are two men wearing navy uniforms. The half of me that's relieved to be saved waves back, but I struggle to hold onto my smile against the sensation of a rope tightening around my throat.

They lower a dinghy and two SAR men motor over to *Sassy*. When they're alongside, they grab a remaining lifeline so the boats bob in unison.

Drew shakes their hands. "Thanks, guys. Thanks for coming to get us."

"All in a day's work," one of the men jokes through a bushy white beard.

"We weren't sure we'd ever see another human being again. Thank you," I say and press a smile to my lips. "Will you be able to tow my boat back?"

"'Fraid not." The bearded man turns to Drew as if he's the owner of *Sassy*. "Sorry, mate." Neither see my collapsing smile or how my hand grabs at my throat.

I stumble through the companionway to hide my fractured face and mumble, "Got to fetch a bag."

The cabin smudges. I hiccup down small sobs, place the remaining money into the backpack, add Drew's drawings, the photo of Bridie, and my father's letters. I collapse against the bunk, strap a hand to my mouth to trap the growing sob. Above, the SAR men hoot with laughter. I swallow hard and move through the cabin, stroking *Sassy*. "Bye, old girl. And thanks."

Leaving her is harder than fighting any storm at sea.

I set my jaw against the AIS alarm that's just gone off inside me. But when I emerge from the companionway and see Drew's stricken expression, my face slips.

This can't be happening. This can't be happening.

I want to scream so loud and so long, hurl Australia, the Pacific, and ten-story high waves at the heavens so Connor can put up his hands and say, "Sorry."

"It'll be okay," Drew whispers when we lower ourselves into the dinghy.

"Welcome to Australia. My name's William, and this is Rob," the bearded guy says. He shakes my hand so vigorously, my ribs hurt. "We'll soon have you back with your family."

Instantly nauseous, I gape from Drew to William. "My mom is here already?"

"Yup. And your uncle and brother. After the initial sighting ten days ago, they were on red-alert in Townsville. Then the storm came in and we lost you. They flew to the Gold Coast last night after we confirmed your new position."

A crashing sensation rattles through my brain, my ears

214

roar. I steady myself on Drew. Suddenly, the truth of what I must face seems too big. Will my family believe what Connor did? Or will they condemn me?

We reach the rescue boat and climb aboard. The two uniformed men have the words *Australian Border Force* written above their shirt pockets. They stay on deck and don't talk to us while Drew and I are urged below for hot tea. But as the boat maneuvers, I drop my blanket and crash the mug onto the table.

"Shae?" Drew's voice follows me back on deck.

Whirling to get my bearings, I seek out *Sassy Jam*. Tears spill down my cheeks. *Sassy* looks forlorn, abandoned, a shell of herself. How can I leave her after the storms we fought together, after she protected me, kept me company, remained a constant for three months, never faltering?

One minute tilts into another.

Sassy Jam curtseys sorrowfully and my heart tears in two. A thousand moments replay in my mind. I slump against the gunwale and watch her shrink smaller until she's a shimmering lone star on the horizon. Drew has come on deck but keeps his distance, understanding this goodbye is between my best friend and me—*Sassy* had crammed a piece of herself into my soul forever, and forever has no end.

CHAPTER 30

The Gold Coast harbor is surprisingly daunting with its horizon of glass skyscrapers. Beneath hunks of cloud that obliterate the sun, the roads twist and knot together, lines of traffic weave, headlights bob and twirl in the chalky morning light. Living on a boat and then Samoa for three months has changed my perspective—the Gold Coast of Australia may as well be New York City.

William nods at me and Drew, a rope in his hands. The rain from an hour ago gleams on his orange SAR jacket.

We're minutes from docking. From seeing my family. From me being arrested.

Drew stands behind me and curls his arms around my middle. I turn my face to rest a cheek against him. The sunscreen smell of him is so strong it's as if he slept inside a coconut. Above us, helicopters hover, making it impossible to talk. Their presence seems like overkill for a sea rescue.

As the SAR boat draws closer to the harbor, a horde of people gush onto the quay. The crowd grows spikes; microphones are thrust toward us. I stiffen. My ears pulse with quick heartbeats. Several police officers help the Search and Rescue officials push the throng back. Our boat bumps the dock, and the splattered shouts and questions of the press are like garbage tipped all over my body.

All I can focus on are the policemen. There'll be no time with my family. No time to say goodbye to Drew. The urge to run away is so strong, I'm close to taking a flying leap off the back of the boat.

William jumps ashore, turns, and offers a helping hand. I stall, a stubborn horse refusing to move into the race gate. Behind me, Drew takes a deep breath then steps off the boat and reaches for my hand. He somehow finds his toothpaste commercial smile.

The last moments before everything changes again.

"I'm right here." Drew grips my wrist, hooks into my stare as he helps me up beside him. Flurries of *us* memories zip too fast across my vision, as if trying to see inside the windows of an express train as it charges through the station. Soon, they'll be all I have left.

"This way, miss." The three words belong to a policeman suddenly standing next to us. He extends an arm, indicating I should go into a building signposted Surf Lifesaving Club.

I shuffle forward. The officer follows us. A TV presenter talks into a camera.

"In a surprising twist to the search for Shae Love, Drew Vega has just stepped off the missing sailboat, Sassy Jam. This is the final scene in a three-month international police hunt for the boat. Sassy Jam was taken by twenty-three-year-old, Shae Love, who is wanted in connection with the murder of Connor Stratton . . ."

My legs buckle. My body seems to dangle as if I'm no more than a mess of clothes hung on a hook. As Drew supports my weight and ushers me forward, I wonder why the presenter is talking about Drew as if he's famous.

Ahead, through the double doors of a white-tiered building, I locate my family. My mother's sleek auburn hair isn't in its usual neat bun but falls silkily around her cheeks, and she's crying so hard that Uncle Brody is her prop. He lifts his

217

free hand in a wave and smiles. The sun has bleached his hair white-blond and it's longer than when I last saw him, flicking out behind his ears.

A sob shudders through me. Drew whisks me forward. Cameras click and flash. Reporters call out and thrust microphones toward me.

"Shae, are you innocent?" one asks.

"Why did you run away, Shae?"

The doors of the lifesaving club slam behind us, and the shouts of the reporters turn to a low murmur.

Mom falls into me, gripping me too tight. "My precious daughter. I thought I'd lost you forever."

My vision is smudgy; salty tears sting my lips when I open them to speak. "It was self-defense." The words are slabs of concrete on my tongue.

"You're safe, and that's all that matters." But Mom's face falls apart again when it should be smiling, and by the way she swipes at her tears as if they're bugs crawling on her cheeks, it doesn't seem as if that's all that matters.

Two policemen watch me. I glance at Finn. Long, chocolate-brown hair flops across his brow. The corner of his mouth twitches upward. His expression parades worry rather than answers. The fear that's hunkered inside me rises into my throat, making my eyeballs bulge like a terrified horse. My thoughts trip and sprawl as if falling downstairs.

"Am I going to be arrested?" I direct my question at Uncle Brody.

"I've made an arrangement to escort you to the station now for questioning," he says. "But it'll be okay. We'll mount a case for self-defense."

I feel as if I'm snapping in three as my knees buckle. My body careens forward; Uncle Brody and Drew grab me. I clutch at my uncle's arms. "Do they think I did it—murder?"

My uncle's expression is sympathetic, the crinkles around his eyes more pronounced. "You're a suspect, Shae, yes."

I suck in air as if the Earth is running out of oxygen.

Uncle Brody draws in a chunky breath. "It would've helped if you hadn't run away, of course. That made you look guilty."

A weight that had wedged itself between my shoulder blades digs deeper. My face puckers. I check my mother, who seems spaced out. Tears gloss her cheeks as her hands make fists. Her mouth opens, then closes. She tries a smile, but it kinks. She leans into Uncle Brody and he wraps his arms around her.

Struggling not to cry, I twist to Drew. He lays a palm on my back. I take his hand. "This is Drew," I say. "We met . . . along the way."

Finn throws on a small grin, then slaps Drew on the back. Uncle Brody nods over Mom's shoulder. Mom turns to Drew, but her smile is somehow pointy.

One of the uniformed border control men approaches, carrying a clipboard. "I have your details, miss," he says to me, then uses his teeth to pull the lid off a pen. "Son?" He spins on his heels to Drew. "I need you to confirm your name, address, and date of birth for the customs form that's mandatory by law. We'll require formal photo identification before you can leave." He waits, pen poised over his clipboard.

Drew frowns, shifts his weight to his other foot. "It's Drew. Drew Vega. You can probably put in a call to my father's office, and his PA will sort out the paperwork you need."

The official's brows shoot up. "*The* Drew Vega?" Drew stares at his bare feet. The man caps his pen. "Right. I'll put a call in, then."

"Drew Vega?" Uncle Brody sputters. "Son of *Anthony* Vega?"

"That'll be me," Drew answers, looking unhappy about the fact.

Finn snorts. "You hit the jackpot there, sis."

My confused gaze swoops to Drew.

"Can we have a minute?" Drew asks. He takes my hand and strides toward the back of the building. "I'm sorry I wasn't completely open about my father. I told you enough, but not the full extent of it. People treat you differently when they know you're the son of an international business magnate."

I recall what Brett said about Drew struggling to find someone who didn't love him for his inheritance.

"I don't even know who Anthony Vega is."

"He's a pretty well-known businessman, the Australian version of Warren Buffet. He's kind of a powerful man."

"And that's why he wants you to take over his business. And because of me, you've had to return to Australia. You'll have to face the music with your father."

Drew chuckles and rubs the back of his neck. "That's okay. Because of you, I'm ready to do that. Although braving my father might be more frightening than fighting a cyclone at sea."

I retrieve my hand from his. "A part of me hoped somehow I'd be acquitted—like they'd somehow know it was an accident. But I'm going to be arrested, Drew. I could be in court, then prison, for years. You must go on with your life. Without me."

"Not going to happen." Drew clutches my arms. "We've already been over this. I'll be there for you. All the way."

"I know we discussed it. But now it's real. I can't do this to you. I can't do this to myself. We have to forget any idea of a future together."

The low murmur of reporters outside the double doors abruptly turns into a round of shouts and calls. I can't quite make out what they're saying.

"Let me in, my good man," a voice says on the other side

of the door. It seems familiar. "I have the paperwork you require for Drew Vega. *Anthony Vega's* son?"

"Sir, you'll have to wait here a moment."

The doors open and a police officer enters, but behind him, Brett looms. When he sees me and Drew, he grins and waves a folder, then pushes into the room. Following him in, is a very tall, beautiful blond woman, more of a goddess. *Another of Brett's girlfriends . . . victims?*

Once Brett hands the folder over to the official with the clipboard, Brett swoops on me, engulfing me in a hug. I can't believe he's ignored Drew.

Into Brett's ear, I whisper, "Kidnapped or not, this is the last time you touch me. Leave. Me. Alone."

"I didn't tell the police," he whispers back. "I promise you. They spotted your boat. That's how they knew. It wasn't me. I gave up a million bucks for you. I could've charged big bucks for TV interviews, too. But I didn't. Because I want you. I adore you, Gotta Go Girl."

I pull away from his embrace and, wondering why Drew isn't stepping in, I cut to him. But Drew's not paying me and Brett any attention. Instead, he's staring at something the blond goddess is holding, and the goddess is staring right back at Drew. I can feel the strong connection between them.

"Ava wanted to come along too, Drew," Brett says.

The goddess takes a few steps closer, and I realize she's cradling a baby bundled in a navy blanket.

"I named him Drew." Ava's smile is slightly smug. "I never stopped loving you, even after you left without so much as a goodbye."

I stiffen and watch Drew do the same.

"I didn't know," he finally murmurs. His focus moves back to the baby, and his mouth twists. I remember what he said at The Trench about being a better dad than his was. Drew glances between the baby and me. In that one look, I know Drew's future is with Ava and his son.

"You didn't answer your phone or emails," Ava adds.

The double doors bang open again, and this time two police officers march in and immediately sight me. One places a hand on my arm. "I'm arresting you for the murder of Connor Stratton—"

"Wait," Uncle Brody jumps in. "I'm her legal representative. I've organized for Miss Love to come in for questioning without being arrested."

The second policeman hands him a document. "We have a warrant for her provisional arrest pending an extradition order from the Office of International Affairs." The color drains from Uncle Brody's face as he reads the paperwork, and the police officer leads me out of the building.

"Shae," Drew shouts from behind me, "I'll be with you . . . all the way."

I pass Ava near the doorway and glimpse the face of the sleeping baby, then look at Drew over my shoulder. "Don't visit. Don't call. Don't write. Forget me. I don't want to see you ever again."

To love him is to let him go.

I recall the three white blossoms floating on a vast black sea, signifying my hope for land and safety nearby. One by one, they sink, swallowed into the depths of the ocean.

CHAPTER 31

Drew

The light in the room suddenly seems to dim. I watch Shae leave, followed by her family. I want to run after her, pull her into my arms and kiss her until she forgets everything but us.

The doors close, and the pressure of a hand on my shoulder snaps me out of the moment. I turn and face Ava. She's smiling, as if it's all going to be how it once was. But we split up just before I took off last year because like every girl I ever meet, she loved the spotlight I provided. The inheritance didn't hurt, even if she was from a wealthy family. How can she think we can pick up where we left off, after everything she and my father did behind my back?

Except now there's a baby.

I look at the face of my son. My heart cramps—there's a gush of affection, of promises never to let him down or force him to be what he is not. I vow to spend time with him so he never feels unimportant. I don't know much about babies, but he looks small and weak for a baby that must be at least four months old. My body rushes with the primal need to protect him.

"Was he premature?" I ask, unable to look directly at Ava.

"No. He's normal and healthy. I'm not going to lie to you, Drew . . . My parents have thrown me out, and I know you still love me. I know we can make this work. But there are DNA tests and the fact he was born six weeks ago. He's not yours, Drew. But if you love me as I love you—"

I cut to her face, then Brett's. He looks pleased with himself. He knew exactly what he was doing when he brought Ava with him today. He thinks she's another stray dog I'm going to rescue, just as I'm always rescuing him.

"Good to see ya, bro," Brett drawls. "I knew you'd make it onto her boat. But I didn't tell anyone where you were, or about Shae. Except your dad when I flew into Sydney. He sent us in his helicopter with your passport. I brought it back from Samoa for you. Ready to leave whenever you are, mate. We can go party in Sydney tonight and—"

"Brett, I regretted hitting you once," I grit out. "But I'll do it again if you ever come near me or Shae ever again."

And then I rush for the doors.

There are two police officers standing outside and a group of reporters. I push between them. Someone yells that I can't leave yet. I surge ahead, weaving through people until a reporter recognizes me.

"Drew Vega. What were you doing on the boat with Miss Love?"

The crowd turns on me, shoving microphones in my face and shouting questions.

"Mr. Vega, did you know Connor Stratton?"

"How did you meet Miss Love? Were you involved in Stratton's death?"

I yell for Shae, but they're a seething wall, blocking me in their circle. Over their heads, I catch my last glimpse of her being herded into a police car.

FOR THREE DAYS, I camp out at the police station. On the first day, they inform me that Shae refuses to see me and then that she's been released into the custody of her uncle. I wait anyway, hoping Brody or Finn will come by. The only time I leave is to buy a new iPhone to be able to follow the news reports about her. Desperate, I send the invoice to my father's PA.

Brett sends me a text.

I'll make you regret dumping me.

But for once, I can't put Brett first, and I ignore him.

Later that day, I learn from the news feeds that Shae and her family were covertly taken to the airport via police escort. She boarded a flight to Sydney this morning, from where she'll fly to America.

A new promise forms in my mind.

I'm coming, Shae.

Continue with **THE FORBIDDEN TIDE**, Book Two in T.M. Bashford's Tide Serial.

More than anything, it would help this early-career author if you left a review for The Heartless Tide as it means I get to keep writing because more reviews mean more people will read my work.

PRAISE FOR BECOMING SIENNA

"I thought the ending was genius!" *Zoe Bentley, Avid Romance Reader*

"Bittersweet and definitely left me wanting more . . . This was a really interesting take on a stalker themed story." *Allyssa O'Brien, Goodreads Reviewer and Between the Spine Blog*

"I absolutely loved the storyline . . . we see growth in Sienna, and the gradual peeling back of her story with her sister Keely was masterfully done." *Laura Hockley, Romance Beta Reader*

"Visual, colorful and emotional . . . the story is captivating right from the start . . . once I started reading, I didn't want to put it down." *Author/Illustrator, Sandra Severgnini*

ABOUT THE AUTHOR

T.M. Bashford is the author of both romantic suspense and young adult novels. First published by Pan Macmillan and Skyhorse Publishing in 2018, in order to go to more book launches, Taryn just moved from the beach to the city with a family that includes teen children and a highly-strung dog who loves cheese.

She's lived on four continents, meaning her job experience has been . . . interesting—an advertising sales rep, a ski chalet chef, a late-night news reader for the BBC, and the CEO of an internet company, but writing is her true love.

As if she doesn't have enough on her plate, she's about halfway through her PhD in Creative Writing while tutoring undergraduates. When she's not writing or teaching creative writing, she's training for triathlons in the hope they will compensate for the fact she spends ten hours a day sat on her tushie.

Learn more about Taryn at www.tmbashford.com or join thousands of readers and sign up for her monthly newsletter which includes bookish giveaways, bookish chat and next book release dates.

For more updates and books you can find T.M. Bashford on Facebook, Instagram and Goodreads

ACKNOWLEDGMENTS

Writing a book is half the journey. Once it's finished, the other half of that journey begins. Both are awesome and inspiring yet scary and difficult roads, but the reward at the end, on seeing that book out in the world, is greater than any gift that could ever be given. Luckily, it's a journey I don't have to take alone.

I'd like to thank my publishing team, especially my editor and my cover designer. There are too many beta readers to name, and there's also my writing group, SWWiG (we mostly drink tea, promise), and my romance critique and support groups. To all of you—*hugs*. Thank you also to Mark Dawson, Alessandra Torre, Dave Chesson and Joanna Penn for your wise advice via courses and podcasts. A special thanks to my mom. Your eagle eye and tireless backing is very much appreciated – and needed.

Of course, without my family letting me escape into my writing room for hours each day, nothing would get written. So, thank for not only understanding and supporting my passion, but for letting me go on book tours, conferences and publishing courses, too. One day, I'll buy you all Porsches. Or maybe pooches. We'll have to see . . .